KEEP MARS WEIRD

ALSO BY NEAL POLLACK

FICTION

Jewball

Never Mind the Pollacks: A Rock and Roll Novel

Beneath the Axis of Evil

The Neal Pollack Anthology of American Literature

Repeat

THE MATT BOLSTER YOGA MYSTERIES

Open Your Heart

Downward-Facing Death

NONFICTION

Stretch

Alternadad

KEEP MARS WEIRD

NEAL POLLACK

47NORTH

Published by 47North, Seattle

www.apub.com

ISBN-13: 9781503951471
ISBN-10: 1503951472

Cover design by Ray Lundgren
Illustrated by David Palumbo

Printed in the United States of America

1

The children were so happy. They loved their life on Earth. Their little faces, the color of fair-trade coffee cut with a tablespoon of almond milk and maybe just a little too much natural sweetener, glowed with health, the product of sound nutrition and lots of outside time. There were fifteen of them, the maximum class size allowed by the Global Education Conference. Arms around one another's shoulders, which was how it was always done in Afternoon Song Circle, they sang:

We never fight.
We never steal.
We never are unkind.
We help our fellow humans
When they are in a bind.
All people are united
Without nation or flag . . .

Jordan Kincaid stood in the middle of the circle, smiling happily, out of professional obligation.

The song ended.

"That was beautiful, kids," Jordan said, following the script. "We must love each other and the Earth to be happy."

The script said that they had to learn the virtues of World Cooperation and Careful Planning. Jordan agreed with the political sentiment, though he found the official language a little syrupy. The greed and violence of the past, which had reduced the human population to a very manageable one billion people, must never be repeated. The days of Omani slave massacres, food-riot YouTubes, and people taking selfies while doing CrossFit could never return. After some dark centuries, at last, humankind had eliminated inequality. Everyone needed to be reminded of that, every day, lest poverty threaten to return. It all had to be nipped in the seedbed.

"Now then, class, what does everybody have?" Jordan asked.

"*Enough!*" the kids said.

"What's that?"

"*Just Enough! No more!*"

The bell rang.

"That's all," Jordan said. "It's been a pleasure teaching you. Have a good—"

The kids were bailing before Jordan could finish, barely even looking at him. They didn't want to be in school any more than he did. Now they were free for six months to do restorative yoga or play chess or go to noncompetitive tree-climbing camp. Most likely, though, they'd sit around watching their Devices.

Jordan, also, was free. Forever. He'd just completed the last day of the last year of his five-year mandated government service. He could select his own career now. He might stay with teaching. It was a very respected profession. Teachers made as much as regenerative cyber-neurosurgeons and almost as much as patent attorneys.

Or he could do something else. Anything, really. He had a powerful mother who owned a 2,200-square-foot house. Maybe he'd just move into her place and read and write and watch his Device. He could volunteer a couple of days a week at the sustainable-aquaculture co-op and get on the board of a couple of cultural festivals, just to make it look like he was busy.

That was the best thing about Earth in 2650. Everybody had Enough, so they could do whatever they wanted with their lives once they'd met their obligations. And Jordan had more Enough than most people. He walked out of the empty classroom, leaving all his papers behind. His real life on Earth had begun.

Two doors down, Daril sat at her desk, sucking on an Organic Cherry Nutri-Pop, which she said she preferred over actual food. Daril had been genetically bred: one-third Brazilian, one-third Filipina, one-third Navajo. She looked good.

Jordan had invited Daril out a bunch of times before she said yes. The very fact that she denied him what he wanted most made him love her all the more. She was right for him. He even thought about marrying her sometimes.

"Hey, Daril," he said as he leaned in the doorframe.

"Jordan," she said, smacking her lolly. "Congratulations. You're free!"

She walked over and gave him a kiss on the cheek, which made his knees so weak he had to grab hold of the doorframe with both hands. He couldn't have been more surprised if she'd stuck her hand down his pants. Thus far she'd only let him hold her hand at an Electric World Orchestra concert.

"How does it feel?" she said. "To be free?"

Was she talking to him? He just wanted to make out. His cheeks felt hot. "Strange," he managed.

So what was the deal in this new, post-cheek-kiss landscape?

Did he get to kiss *her* now?

"You're lucky," she said. "I have two more years of this crap."

She didn't *seem* to be expecting or desiring a kiss from him. She seemed pretty focused on her career. Love was such a thrill ride.

"Lucky?" Jordan said. "Huh. I have no idea what I'm going to do with my life."

"Who does?"

"Or who I'm going to do it with," he added coyly.

"You flirt!"

This excited him.

Then she said, "How is your *excellent* mother?" which excited him less.

"She's doing fine," Jordan said.

"I just love those parties she throws."

Jordan had taken Daril to several of his mother's quarterly salons. They'd been fun enough, though the two of them rarely left together. Daril made friends so easily.

"The people at them are so interesting," she said. "Unlike the people in my everyday life, who are so boring."

"I'm not so boring," Jordan said.

Daril didn't exactly reply to that. "Well," she said instead, "you *are* lucky to have been born into a very important family. My father was an egg farmer."

"Whoever your father was, he raised you perfectly."

"Sure he did."

"Maybe we could have dinner tonight?" Jordan said. "They're serving yellow lentils at the Ethiopian Cafeteria. Or we could go to Little Vietnam and have a sustainably farmed catfish hotpot."

Jordan had made reservations at both. Even before she'd kissed him, he'd had big plans for this evening. After dinner, he intended to surprise Daril with a weekend at a hot-tub resort in the Himalayan foothills, which could only be accessed via hyperloop. Then they'd take psilocybin and things would get interdimensionally orgasmic.

"Not tonight," she said.

"Please," he said.

"Jordan . . ."

"Daril, I really really want to spend time with you. I think we—"

"Jordan, I'm flattered. But I'm wiped. It's been a long school year, and I just want to sit in a gel tube and watch stories on my Device. Alone. By myself. For a while. Maybe for weeks."

Jordan thought that he must have looked very despondent, because she kissed him on the cheek again. This one didn't have the same effect as the first one, though. Now it just seemed like a pity kiss.

"Don't be sad," she said. "You're sweet. Any girl or guy or polyamorous sex commune would be so lucky to end up with you."

Jordan sulked away, knowing he was beaten, and left the school without looking back. The number 3 solar-powered driverless über-bus pulled up in front as if it had been summoned to haul his defeated carcass away. Jordan trudged onboard and swiped his transit pass, which was free to all young people engaged in World Service.

It was a glorious spring afternoon in Austin, like all afternoons had been since the defeat of the oil cartels in the great Climate Change Reversal War. Austin was one of the few large cities that had come out ahead in the Days of Weather. Through various acts of fate and history, it had been a temperate coastal metropolis for the last 350 years.

The bus glided down the beautiful, tree-lined, traffic-free, pedestrian- and bike-friendly avenues. With the windows open, Jordan could hear the Mexican Ocean gently crashing onto the shores of Town Beach, punctuated by the happy shouts of well-paid professional surfers. They passed by Clinton Warrior Plaza, cruised past the headquarters of Hexagram and Winkle, dipped under the High Line and over the Low Line, skirted the edge of the ganja district, and circled the restaurant-supply hangars. Jordan pulled the cord when they reached Mixed-Use Village. The driverless bus stopped in front of his high-rise.

Jordan got off, jobless, girlfriendless, and life-missionless. Gaia damn it, this was his last day of Service! He deserved to celebrate. Instead, he had to pay a bunch of resort cancellation fees.

As he rode the elevator to his decent apartment, Jordan Kincaid asked himself the question that's plagued moderately intelligent and improbably prosperous young people since the dawn of civilization:

What now?

2

Jordan's roommate, Leonard Tolliver, sat in the living room of their fifteenth-floor apartment, which had two bedrooms and a composter that fed into the building's Central Composting Unit, which itself fed into a larger Composting Unit for the block. The compost was then used in the Neighborhood Farm that grew the vegetables and herbs and provided the feed for the Sustainable Aquaculture and Free Range Chicken Unit, as well as the potting soil for the ganja district. So, in a way, Leonard was always working for the greater good, even when he wasn't working.

He'd very recently completed his own five-year service, as a seed-hydration supervisor in the ganja district's third largest grow bank. Before that, he'd graduated summa cum laude from the University of Austin's prestigious Willie Nelson School of Natural Pharmaceuticals. He'd worked nearly twenty hours a week, thirty weeks a year, for the better part of a decade. Enough already.

It was time to kick back.

Leonard opened his special box, constructed from pure 100 percent synthetic hemp fiber, temperature and moisture controlled via app or voice command. He pressed a button. Four shelves emerged from the box like scarves from a magician's hat.

"Hello, my sweets," he said.

One shelf contained several fat nugs of Smelly Nelly, Leonard's favorite super-indica for when it was time to forget his problems. Another held all chocolates and candies and breath mints and sprays, accumulated over many years of toil in the Natural Pharma sector. The third shelf was for gear—pipes, picks, screens, sonic dewaxers, and the like. The fourth contained what Leonard was looking for: a fat syringe, filled with a hundred milligrams of high-octane sativa THC liquid.

Leonard took the syringe out of the box and looked at it lovingly.

"And you, my dear," he said, "are the sweetest one of all."

Leonard walked into the kitchen and pressed a few buttons on the food combinator. Molecules arranged themselves. The combinator beeped. Leonard pressed the chill button. Five seconds, and it beeped again.

He opened it up and pulled out a plump mango, at the peak of ripeness.

"Every queen needs a carriage," he said.

He stuck the needle into the mango and filled the fruit with cannajuice. Natural compounds in the mango increased the potency of the cannabinoids. That was Pharma-Chemistry 101, a class that Leonard had passed with a flying A.

He took a lush bite out of the mango. Within seconds, he was wondrously high. He went back into the living room and turned on his Device. Adult Swim, the most popular network for hundreds of years, came on.

Cool, it was Ideology Bear.

"Education is bad for you," Ideology Bear said. "A yup a yup a yup."

Leonard laughed out loud. "So subversive," he said.

Jordan walked in.

"What's up, Mr. Chips?" Leonard said. He had an inexhaustible memory for pop culture trivia, spanning back a thousand years.

Jordan sighed.

Leonard extended the mango to Jordan. "Fruit of the vine!" he said.

"Is that cannafruit?" Jordan said.

"Nothing but the finest."

"No thanks. It makes me tired."

"Suit yourself," said Leonard. He took another juicy bite.

Jordan began walking around, opening curtains and windows. World Congress said that natural light was the best mood enhancer, second only to fresh sea air, so most habitations had ample access to both. Leonard didn't buy it. He hissed like a vampire.

"Stop!" he said.

"It stinks in here," Jordan said.

"I like to marinate."

"Uch."

"Come on, this is a huge day for us! We are *done*, dude!"

Leonard and Jordan had been best friends for more than twenty years. They'd grown up in the same neighborhood and had served in the same Junior Achievement Scout pod. Once, on vacation, they'd almost drowned together in the Sea of Guatemala. And now they were men, in search of adulthood.

Jordan slumped in his hover-chair and raked his hands through his hair. "I don't feel so good," he said.

"Uh-oh," said Leonard. "What's the matter, buddy?"

"It's Daril," Jordan said. "I had this big date planned."

"Daril is lame."

"I think about her, and then I think about her some more," Jordan said.

"Stop obsessing."

"I can't help it."

"Are you crying?" Leonard said.

Jordan was. It was socially acceptable for people of all genders to express emotions however they wanted. Except for anger, which needed to be controlled.

"What is the point of life, Leonard?" Jordan said. "Why are we here? What are we going to do next?"

"I don't know, man. We'll figure it out. We should enjoy! This is the moment that we wanted. Our obligations are over."

"They are never over."

"But they *are.* Now we have Enough."

"I don't have Daril."

"You need to have some Smelly Nelly."

"I'm not really a weed man, Leonard, you know that."

"It'll help you relax. Forget your problems."

Jordan snuffled. "I don't have any problems," he said. "At least not any that weed can solve."

He went to his bedroom. There, on his nightstand, sat a photo of him and Daril at one of his mother's parties. True, they stood ten feet apart, but they'd been in the same house for almost two hours that night. That had been quite a breakthrough.

He lay down on his bed and turned the sleep setting to "deep afternoon nap." The bed began to vibrate gently and to hum a sweet lullaby. Jordan had had a tough day, but nothing was more important than adequate rest. He fell asleep quickly.

♦ ♦ ♦

When Jordan opened his eyes, it was dark outside. He'd slept for a long time, and he felt better. The night and even his life had possibility.

He got up and went into the kitchen. The smartlights automatically came on at about a third of their power. Jordan waved his hand, and the teakettle began boiling repurposed wastewater. The windows were all still open; Leonard was out somewhere. From a distance, five blocks away at Town Beach, Jordan could hear music, the Friday Night Concert. He went over to the window. It sounded like Bach, something challenging and enriching, but also pleasant. Later, there'd be a Nicki Minaj tribute band. Some music was just too legendary to die.

The kettle dinged. Jordan poured a cup and went back to the window. He sipped his organic tea, felt the gentle breezes on his face, and listened to the soft music. He felt calm, peaceful, and undisturbed. This was the peak of his youth. Daril had rejected him, but only temporarily. Soon, he'd find the cherry-flavored key to her heart.

All was perfection.

The door burst open.

Leonard came through, accompanied by a guy who was wearing a top hat, a monocle, and a black waistcoat, as well as hip-hugging black jeans, tightly laced black boots that went up to the knee, and a white frilly shirt that was open three buttons, revealing a manly tuft of hair. This was not a World Congress–issue outfit. Jordan doubted it had been manufactured sustainably.

"Dude!" Leonard said. "Look who I found at the tavern!"

"Who?" Jordan said.

He looked at the guy, who had a soul patch and a curlicued mustache, which had obviously been slicked and waxed.

"This guy!" Leonard said.

"I don't know who this guy is," said Jordan.

"You don't recognize him?"

"No."

Leonard and the guy laughed conspiratorially. The guy covered up his mustache with his hands. Jordan still didn't recognize him. Then the guy let the monocle drop. Finally, he removed his top hat.

"Oh my God!" Jordan said. "Dave Waters!"

Dave Waters had been their boyhood friend. He'd disappeared around eighth level. His father had been a profiteer, which wasn't illegal but was frowned upon and heavily regulated. Austin was no place for a person to make a buck and then not share the wealth. The Waters family left. They hadn't heard from Dave since.

"Where have you been?" Jordan said.

"Dude," Dave Waters said. "I've been partying on Mars. Nonstop. My dad runs the Martian Development Corporation. We cruised up there. This is the first time we've been back in like years."

Jordan was skeptical. Mars, he'd always thought, was for bachelor parties. As much as he doubted his place on the Earth sometimes, he never wanted to leave it. But Leonard did. He talked about Mars all the time.

"What's it like up there?" Leonard asked. "What is it *really* like?"

"There are clubs that never close!" Dave Waters said. "It's a nonstop party, and people can wear whatever they want. I know a lot of really cool people, and we're always just having the best time. It's pretty chill overall."

"Mars, man," Leonard said. "Fucking Mars. Can you believe it? Our old friend Dave Waters is a *Martian.*"

"Earth-Martian," Dave corrected him. "Big difference. The actual Martians live . . . somewhere else."

"Whatever, man, you are from *Mars.* That is so great," Leonard said. "I bet our little Earth apartments don't seem like much to you."

"Naw, it's all good," Dave said. "I like Earth. It's relaxing in a really Earth way."

Dave was looking at Leonard expectantly.

Jordan read the signals.

"Leonard," Jordan said, "don't keep our guest waiting."

"Oh, right, dude, sorry," Leonard said. "Have a seat."

Leonard produced one of his endless series of nugs, did the grind-and-load, and offered Dave Waters the aqua-bong.

"I'm honored to present you the Green Hit," he said.

Dave took a massive pull and passed it over to Leonard, who gave Jordan a "Want some?" look. Jordan shook his head.

"Mars, man," said Leonard. "It sounds way better than Earth. The culture is so stale here."

"Yeah, Earth is pretty lame," Dave agreed. "But it's relaxing for a week or two, and at least you can go for a mountain hike without being torn to shreds by a solar storm."

"Sometimes I just want to get out of here and go to Mars and just hang out," Leonard said. "Check out the scene. You know. Live someplace different. Try it out."

"I totally love it," Dave said. "Anything can happen on Mars, anytime. There are festivals every week. The main one goes on for three months."

"Keep Mars Weird," Leonard said. "That's what they say. Right?"

"Right," Dave said, without much enthusiasm.

"I've always wondered," Jordan said. "What exactly is so weird about Mars? And why does it need to be kept that way?"

"I don't know, it's just unusual and strange," said Dave. "And that's pretty cool."

"But does everyone have Enough?" Jordan asked.

"Enough what?"

"Enough clean water. Enough space to live. Enough satisfying work. Enough intellectual stimulation. Enough access to public transportation and free, good-quality health care. All those things that make life worthwhile. That so many people on Earth fought and died for over hundreds of years."

"I don't know," Dave said.

"What do you mean, you don't know?"

"People on Mars aren't really into that kind of stuff."

"What do you mean? That's not 'stuff.' Those are *human rights.*"

Dave shrugged and grinned. "Keep Mars Weird," he said, as though that were any kind of answer.

3

Leonard and Dave got louder and louder and more and more baked. Jordan found himself developing some second hand munchies. It happened, living with Leonard.

Through the haze, they were watching *The Incredible Holographic Mangapus*, a stylized cartoon symbolizing Japan's pride in rescuing itself by building elevated islands. The Mangapus's many 3-D tentacles whipped around, making the room glow bright purple.

"Whoa," Dave said. "The Mangapus totally got me!"

"Save me, Captain Protodelicious!" said Leonard.

Seeing this legendary anime gave Jordan an idea.

"You guys wanna go grab some ramen?" he said.

Ramen was everyone's favorite weekend treat. All sectors had a communal noodle kitchen. They were always packed, especially on Friday nights, when the lines stretched for several blocks by 8:00 p.m. But the youthful, energetic residents of Austin had no problem waiting in line for an awesome and relatively inexpensive dinner. They were just all so happy to be living in the world's greatest city.

Soon enough, in just under three hours, the three friends were sitting at a two-hundred-person communal table, slurping on organic pork broth with buckwheat noodles, seaweed, and sustainable eggs.

"Dude, this is so good," Dave said. "You cannot get ramen this good on Mars."

"I'm sure Mars has decent food," Jordan said.

"It has its own thing going on, for sure," said Dave, "but food can get really controversial."

"What do you mean, controversial?" Jordan said.

"People get hungry and complain. Because they're takers."

"But hunger has been eradicated," Jordan said in response to this repulsively shocking political sentiment. "Everyone always has Enough food, as much as they need. It's the law."

"The law," Dave said. "Right."

"Dude," said Leonard, always apolitical. "Check this out."

He'd put one noodle up each nostril. When he was sure he had their attention, he snorted hard, and they disappeared. Then he coughed them out his mouth.

The young women sitting next to him recoiled and fled.

"Harsh, ladies," Leonard called after them.

"Leonard, you should come party with us on Mars," Dave said. "You'd have a blast."

"I'd love to," said Leonard. "But I don't have any Launchpad cash right now."

"Man, I'll totally bankroll you."

"Seriously?"

Jordan found the conversation less than stimulating. He glanced around the room, and his eye caught someone familiar coming through the door. Could it be?

She walked in a couple of steps.

It was!

Daril!

She'd decided to join him for dinner after all. He was glad he'd enabled his Geo-Location Chip for her. The only other people who had his coordinates were his mother and Leonard, who needed him sometimes when he got locked out of the apartment. Even though Jordan was halfway done with his soup, he'd gladly order another bowl, or even a dish of kimchi sprouts, so he could spend an hour in Daril's company.

She waved, her eyes brightening.

He waved back at her.

"You guys," he said. "My future wife is here."

"Where?" said Dave.

"She's coming over," he said.

Daril walked straight past them.

At the other end of the dining hall, a big guy stood up. He was muscular, probably an isometrics major. Daril ran toward him, squealing, and leapt into his arms.

"Looks like your future wife has got a date," Leonard said.

"It's probably her cousin or something," said Jordan.

Daril's "cousin" had his tongue halfway down her throat and his hand firmly planted on her ass.

"Well, they're definitely close," said Dave.

"I should probably go talk to her," Jordan said.

Leonard slid Jordan a cup of sake.

"You'll need this," he said.

Jordan slugged it. He walked over. Daril was next to the lunk. They were holding hands across the table.

"Hey, Daril," he said.

She looked at him, eyes wide.

"Jordan!" she said. "I . . . I . . . I thought . . ."

"I just wanted to meet your friend," Jordan said.

Jordan extended a hand. "Jordan Kincaid," he said.

"Andrei," the guy said, a little confused.

"Daril is my—"

"Jordan and I work together," she said. "*Worked* together. His service ended today."

"Congratulations," Andrei grunted.

"It's more than a work relationship," Jordan said.

"Is it now?" Andrei said.

"Jordan and I are very close friends," said Daril.

"We've already been to several parties together," Jordan said.

"Jordan is from an important family," she said.

"I would like to make you part of that family," he said.

Andrei might've laughed a little.

Daril sighed. "Look, Jordan," she said. "You're a nice guy, and you're an OK teacher, but we're not . . . we've never been . . ." She shook her head and tried again. "I like to spend my time with *men*, Jordan. And sometimes women. But mostly men. Who are strong. And forceful."

"I can be strong."

"Jordan, we are *not* a couple."

"Daril, you don't mean it."

But she did. Jordan had no choice but to slink away. He felt his heart cracking. How was this possible? How could Daril betray him like this?

"That went well," said Leonard.

"It's not her," Jordan said. "It's the guy she's with. He poisoned her. Put altered pheromones into her water supply or something."

"Right," Leonard said.

"Dude," said Dave. "Don't sweat it. That chick isn't even hot by Mars standards."

"But I don't want Mars standards," said Jordan. "I want Daril."

"Relax," said Leonard. "It's just a woman. Try crushing on another gender. There are lots of choices."

"No, she is not just a woman! She's . . . she's . . ."

He looked over to Daril's table. She and Andrei were entwined like vines. Andrei was licking her neck.

"I need more sake," Jordan said.

They ordered a bottle. It came on ice. Jordan bolted it down. He ordered another. That also went down his gullet.

"Slow down, amigo," said Leonard. Usually, he encouraged partying, but this was obviously something else.

"Why should I?" said Jordan. "It's Friday night, and"—he cupped his hands to his mouth and raised his voice—"*apparently I can do whatever I want*!"

"Oh boy," Leonard said.

"Waiter!" Jordan shouted. "More sake! Two more sakes!"

Fifteen minutes later, Jordan rose from his seat and belched fermented rice.

"Now they'll see what a strong and forceful man can be," he said, hiccupping.

"Hey, man," Leonard said. "Maybe you should just sit and relax. Just be cool and nice."

"No," Jordan said, his voice slurring. "I've been too nice for too long."

"That's certainly true."

"I'm gonna go stand up for my woman."

Jordan staggered over to where Daril and Andrei were mooning at each other, hands joined over the table. He tapped Andrei on the shoulder.

"Hey," he said.

Andrei ignored him. Daril looked in the other direction.

"Hey, I am talking to you, meat pie!"

Andrei turned around. "Do we have a problem, brother Jordan?"

"Yes, I do believe that we do indeed have a problem right here," Jordan said. "Right now we definitely have a problem, and that problem is that you are molesting my future wife, Daril."

"Go away," Andrei said. "You're drunk."

"*You're* drunk, asshole!"

"No, I'm not."

"Whore of Gaia!" Jordan shouted.

He shoved Andrei, in the back. Ramen splattered across the table.

"I will crush your face!" Jordan cried.

"Oh my God, Jordan," Daril said. "Stop."

"Why should I stop?" he said, shoving Andrei again. "I will never stop loving you, Daril."

Andrei stood, his bulk looming ominously, a great tower of sustainable, grass-fed meat. Jordan staggered back, bumping into the counter behind him. He was wiry and fit, as mandated by law, but Andrei was a slab of pure power.

"Maybe you should leave us alone," Andrei said.

People almost never fought anymore. They didn't even have *verbal* conflict. It was the Age of Mutual Consent. But at that moment, something deep inside Jordan slipped away. Never in his life had he been this drunk. He was about to find out why.

"You leave *me* alone!" he howled. "*Aaaaaaaaiieeeeeeeee!*"

He launched himself at Andrei's chest. The surprise knocked Andrei back across the table and into Daril's soup bowl. She yelped as the hot ramen plopped in her lap.

Jordan smacked at Andrei with the sides of his closed fists, making noises like a wet-bottomed pet rodent—*eep, eep, eep*—as he did so. Andrei threw him off like a doll. Jordan smashed into the next table over, turning its diners, their chairs, and the table itself into a howling tangle of limbs, wood, and hot ramen. Andrei stood up, brushed some noodles off his face, and walked toward Jordan, fist grinding into palm.

The restaurant erupted. People were screaming. Behind the counter, a chef texted the police: "Terrible violence has erupted at the communal ramen shop." Leonard and Dave were halfway across the restaurant. They had no way to get through the scrum.

Jordan separated himself from the ruins and backed away on his elbows down the narrow aisle. He didn't get far. Andrei wore thick, very heavy boots. He raised one high and sent its lethal black sole whistling toward Jordan's face. Jordan whipped his head to the side. The other boot came down, grazing Jordan's ear, drawing blood. It made him dizzier than he already was.

Somehow, he found wits enough to scoot on his butt through Andrei's legs, bumping into Daril. She was standing now, staggering around.

He clawed at Daril's ankles.

"Please," he said. "Why won't you love me?"

Andrei picked Jordan up by the collar, spun him around, and pounded his face with a closed fist. Jordan felt something crunch unnaturally below his eye. Blood spurted out of his nose onto Andrei's shirt. Another fist came. Jordan twisted away, and it caught him on the same ravaged ear where he'd been kicked. Andrei picked him up again and launched him across a booth. Jordan hit the back of his head. A photograph, depicting smiling sushi chefs, hit the top of his head, shattering glass everywhere.

There were chopsticks next to him on the table. Jordan grabbed them. As Andrei punched down at him, his face close, his breath hot and angry, Jordan dodged, barely, and thrust the chopsticks upward.

Andrei caught the chopsticks just before they plunged into his right eye. Jordan tried to push them. He wanted to kill this man, wanted to taste his blood, for stealing away Daril. Andrei squeezed Jordan's hand. Jordan could feel the bones start to give way. Jordan reached to his right, grabbed a jar of hot peppers in juice, and smashed Andrei in the head. The jar broke. Andrei's face was covered in pepper juice. He released Jordan's hand. Clawing at his eyes, he howled, "It burrrrrrrns!"

The restaurant was chaos. People scrambled over one another for the exits. Two hover-drones smashed through what remained of the ramen shop's glass front door. They shone a spotlight on Jordan's face. He and Andrei stood next to each other, heaving.

"Stop in the name of the World Congress!" said the hover-drones.

Jordan bowed his head.

Across the shop from the action, Leonard and Dave looked at each other.

"To his credit," Leonard said, "he's still standing."

"Yeah," Dave said, "he actually did pretty well."

As the drones marched Jordan out, he found Leonard in the crowd and yelled, "Call my mother, please!"

Leonard picked up his phone.

"In progress," he called after the departing Jordan. To Dave, Leonard said, "Some welcome back to Earth, huh?"

"No worries," Dave said. "This kind of thing happens on Mars all the time."

4

Jordan Kincaid sat in his soundproof cell at the Austin Rehabilitative Center for Temporary Criminals, feeling glum. He'd been in there for almost thirty-six hours and had only been allowed to cruise the holographic web twice. The medical staff had applied salve and bandages every eight hours instead of the legally required six. Also, the prison served him a tomato salad that wasn't 100 percent fresh, as well as oatmeal that tasted suspiciously instant—both clear violations of the Geneva Beach conventions. His cell only measured about 440 feet, not counting the small water closet, which had a near-empty soap dispenser and a toilet that obviously hadn't been cleaned for days. When they freed him from this hell, there would be a lawsuit.

The doors to the cell whooshed open. There stood a pashmina-clad middle-aged woman, typing frantically on a pad.

"Mother," Jordan said. "Where have you been?"

"The wheels of justice turn slowly," she said. "Let's go."

Jordan's mother was the Cultural Connector for the Americas, a very prominent position. She knew everyone. This meant that she didn't have to take the bus, at least not all the time, a rare privilege reserved for the most important people. There was a solar-powered, self-driving über-limo waiting in front of the jail. They got in.

"Mother—" Jordan began.

"What were you thinking?" she said. "That was the first time someone's been arrested for assault in Austin in six months."

"I was defending Daril's honor."

"Quit your simpering. That woman is a dolt."

"I won't stand to have her called that."

"Well, she is. With those pouty lips and those stupid little heels. But even if she's the finest person in the world, why should she settle for you? You have the potential to make more or less the same money as anyone else. And you're about as macho as a bag of turnips."

"I love her!"

"You think women are waiting around for a man to love them? That idea is as old as Chicago's public transportation system. Everyone is equal, and women are more equal than anyone else. There are officially six different female subgenders, for Gaia's sake. No one *needs* love anymore, at least not from one person, and certainly not from you, Jordan. You have to *offer* a woman something."

"I don't even know what that means," Jordan said.

"Now your father," she said, "*he* was a man. He knew how to thrill me like no one else."

"Mother, please."

"I don't just mean sexually—though there was *plenty* of that, until the day he didn't—but there was adventure and action in his blood. His generation of men *built* things. They created. They schemed. And they looked damn good in dungarees when they did it. They got dirty and they *were* dirty. You and your friends are soft and lazy, Jordan, that's the trouble with you."

Jordan slumped down in the seat of his mother's private über-limo. "Does this thing still have an organic-lemonade dispenser?" he said. "I'm dehydrated."

They arrived at Jordan's mother's house. She lived in one of the few large single-unit dwellings in town. It included a detached solarium in the backyard, where she kept her prize orchids, way more space than one person needed, but she was the Connector and threw salons and dinner parties for dignitaries. It was as much Enough as the World Congress would allow anyone to have.

They went into the solarium. Jordan's mother waved her hand and the tea started brewing.

"Jordan," she said. "We need to have a talk about your future."

"My future is fine, Mother."

"It is out the window."

"What are you talking about?"

"As punishment, they want to sentence you to work at the Device-installation company."

"Gaia no!" Jordan said. "That would be life death."

"That's what I told them," she said. "No son of mine works for a utility. So I made some calls and some arrangements and got you a teaching job."

"That's fine," Jordan said. "I like teaching well enough."

"Out of town."

"In Dallas? Kansas City? Phoenix?"

All those places could easily be reached by high-speed levi-train. He could keep his apartment in Austin.

"Further than that," his mother said.

"Minneapolis? The temperatures barely reach fifty there in the winters. But I can deal, I suppose."

"Not Minneapolis," said Jordan's mother. "New Austin."

"New Austin?" Jordan said. "But that's on—"

"Mars."

"*Mars?*"

"Best I could do."

"That's . . . that's . . . *another planet*!"

"No kidding. I had to pull a lot of strings to even score you a teaching job *there.* Because of you, the judge's daughter gets to be third cello in the Austin Orchestra. She's barely qualified to be *fourth* cello. I just pray that no one notices."

"Not acceptable, Mother."

"Oh, for Gaia's sake," she said. "When your father was your age, *he* went to Mars."

"He did?" Jordan said. "I didn't know that."

"Yes, and he died there, too."

"I thought he died in the Indian Ocean, trying to build an underground symphony palace."

"You were young. New Austin had gotten overcrowded, and they needed architects and engineers to build towers so people there could live like they could on Earth."

She wiped back a tear. Jordan had never seen her cry before.

"He told me he'd be back in time for your tenth birthday. And he was planning to come home, too. I know he was. Then one day I got a transmission from him. I saved it, too. Do you want to see it?"

Jordan didn't, really. The last thing he wanted was to think about his father. He'd spent more or less his entire life without him, listening to stories of his derring-do and heroism. It had been a hard enough couple of days. Jordan didn't need reminders of his inadequacy. Still, he had trouble saying no to his mother.

"Fine," he said.

Jordan's mother fiddled with her Device. Up came the flickering image, which cut in and out, like all transmissions from space. But there he was, Jordan's father, whom Jordan had only seen in stills. He was looking around nervously, like he was worried someone was going to break in the door.

"My darling wife," he said. "I have to go away. For a while. Maybe forever. I may not be coming home at all. What I'm trying to say is that Mars is at a crossroads. Things need to change up here, and the people need to fight. It's bad, it's really bad. It's like Earth was, or at least like I imagine what it was like, only worse. Outside this dome, we're on Mars, and there is nowhere to escape. Except for the other dome, which contains New Waco and New Bakersfield. But no one wants to go to those cities. They are so boring. And then there's the New Francisco dome, which is great, but *no one* can afford that."

She paused the transmission.

"What else does he say?" Jordan asked.

"It's mostly sex stuff. It goes on for another five minutes."

"Ew. Turn it off."

She did.

"I don't *want* to live on Mars," Jordan said.

"In your father's day, people considered it an *honor* to go to Mars. Those young men and women never complained. They were doing it for humanity."

"But—"

"You young people are such special snowflakes," she said. "You've never known winter, or a flood, or a food riot. You've never seen a world where not everyone has Enough."

"Neither have you," Jordan said.

"I've seen plenty, bub," she said.

"Pfft."

"Don't smart off to me, Jordan. I pulled your ass out of that jail. You were going to have to spend an entire week there. A *week.* In *prison. My* son."

"I'm going to appeal."

"You don't get an appeal. You don't have a choice!"

"Please," Jordan said. "I can make this right."

"Your flight leaves in a month. Drop your cocks and grab your socks, boy. You're going to Mars."

5

Jordan's mother offered him the limo home, but Jordan said he'd rather walk. It was fine for her to get carted around like some sort of duchess. He didn't deserve special service.

Jordan turned up the tint on his holo-glasses and stared up toward the sun. It was so warm and welcoming, the sky so clear and blue and fresh. Now he had to leave his earthly paradise for the dark unknown. He wanted comfort and security, not adventure, but adventure is what his drunken actions were going to bring him. *I am a criminal*, he thought. He was getting sent to Mars like some sort of nineteenth-century British thief exiled to Australia.

Leonard was on the couch, watching a two-hundred-year-old *Lucky Ducky* marathon block. Having access to six centuries' worth of cartoons could really take up a guy's time.

"That is just reprehensible," Lucky Ducky sputtered as Jordan came through the door.

"Hey, look who's out of jail!" Leonard said, offering up the aqua-bong. "You want a hit?"

"No," Jordan said. "It makes me tired."

"Suit yourself," Leonard said, then took a long pull.

Jordan had had enough, and not the good kind of Enough.

"You know, Leonard, I'm sick of marijuana. Sick sick sick of it. It's all anyone ever does, and it's all anyone ever talks about."

"Is someone grumpy?" Leonard said.

"And I'm sick of cartoons."

"This one is so much better than the reboot."

"I don't give a shit about reboots! Also, I'm sick of you slacking around all the time. Why don't you grow up and be a responsible citizen, you Gaia-fucking sponge?"

"Whoa, horsey," Leonard said.

Jordan slumped onto the couch. "I'm sorry."

"It's cool, man," said Leonard.

"I just got some really bad news."

"What?"

"You're going to have to find somewhere else to get stoned."

"Yeah, I am."

"You are. Because I'm moving to Mars."

"Me, too."

"I said I'm moving to Mars."

"Yeah, man, so am I. Dave's dad has billions of launch miles. He said I could have a seat on the rocket next month."

"What are you going to *do* on Mars? *I* have a job."

"I don't know. I've got my benefits. They transfer, maybe. I'll figure out something."

"I don't know how I feel about this."

Leonard clapped his arm around Jordan's shoulder. "You should feel pretty good," he said. "We're going to be bros in space! It's an amazing opportunity, to get to go up there together. Mars is incredible. It's the coolest place in the galaxy, by far. The girls are chill, and people are able to just hang out without any rules and be who they really *are.*"

"Yeah, but rules are good."

"Up there, you won't be a criminal," Leonard said. "You'll just be another guy looking for his path."

Dave came walking through the door. He was still wearing his top hat and monocle, but also neon-blue ankle-length shorts and a sleeveless flannel shirt with a purple ostrich feather stuck in the lapel.

"Yolo," Dave said, using a phrase that had somehow endured since its birth at the dawn of the Second Prehistoric Era. It had come to enjoy universal meaning, just like *aloha* had at one time, or *shalom*.

"Yolo," said Leonard. "Great threads!"

"Yeah, it was in my Daily Fashion Update yesterday and I just clicked and ordered," Dave said. "Clothes change all the time on Mars. It's got Style Trends."

Leonard scowled down at his World Congress–issued breathable-fiber unitard. "I wish I had a Daily Fashion Update."

"You can get one on Mars," Dave said. "You can get anything for a price."

"I got my benefits!" Leonard said. "To pay for things."

"Your benefits," said Dave. "Right."

"Hey, guess what? Jordan's going to Mars, too!"

Dave shook his hands in Jordan's direction, a gesture that had been known, in medieval times, as "jazz hands," but had since been ironically appropriated. "Yolo!" he said. He pulled a little canvas bag out of his board shorts. "I got a little treat for you noobs."

"Is that . . ." Leonard said.

"Yes, sir. It is one-hundred-percent, certified-genuine pure Mars Dust, distilled from the Red Planet's finest crystalline soil."

"That's quite a description," Jordan said.

"Oh yeah," said Dave. "It's straight from the ad. You can buy this stuff premium on Mars."

"Well, spark it!" Leonard said.

"You don't spark it," said Dave. "That would kill you. So instead you suck it up your nose. One snort of this shit, and you'll be on Jupiter for lunch."

Dave put a little mound of dust on the table, spread it out, and started separating it using the blade from his Swiss EarthCorps knife.

"It's better if you dose it out," he said.

He leaned in, covered a nostril with an index finger, and sucked a little mound of Mars Dust up through the other nostril.

"*Sonofamother!*" he exclaimed. "That shit is good!"

Jordan was shocked. The International Toxicity Congress had outlawed snortable drugs more than a century ago. Even if they became available on Earth, no one could afford them. The privilege of snorting a mound of space dust could cost up to a year's salary. Who would want to try such a thing?

Leonard leaned in and snorted up a big mound. He threw his head back and howled.

Dave's pupils were the size of Frisbees. Leonard's were expanding as well.

"*Gheeeeeeee*!" they exclaimed.

Dave got up. He started hopping very excitedly.

"You should try some, Jordan," he said. "It's really really really really incredible!"

"No thanks," Jordan said.

Now Leonard was up and hopping, too. "No, no, Jordan," he said. "You really, really should. It's happy happy happy happy. This is Mars Dust we're talking about, man, the stuff of *Mars*. This stuff is legendary. Man, I never thought I'd get to do Mars Dust." He shook his head like a horse shaking off water. "*Whooooooooo*!" he shouted. "I can hear the music. *All* the music."

He and Dave grabbed each other's shoulders and started hopping up and down gleefully.

"Mars!" they chanted. "Mars! Mars! Mars! Mars! Mars!"
Jordan sighed.
His flight to Mars didn't leave for a month.
And he was already tired.

6

Jordan sat in the solar-powered über-bus on the way to the Johnson City spaceport. He'd left behind all his belongings except for a spare unitard, six pairs of underwear, a thousand hydration tablets, a tooth jet, a spare tooth jet, a retractable parka, and a tablet so he could watch his favorite tasteful comedies, the *Nightly Goodnews*, and season six hundred of *Downton Abbey*, as well as read the complete works of William Shakespeare and D'Paula Quillenbush, history's two greatest writers, and maybe also play a few rounds of solitaire and Monkey Jumpy. All this he was able to stuff into a backpack, which was in the overhead container.

There was also a copy of *The World Congress Book of Facts*, that essential text for all primary school students, a completely vetted compendium of science and history, all of it very objective, though geared toward teaching children that Enough is Enough. Jordan had internalized its messages completely, but he still needed to study it carefully on the flight over, because he didn't know where Martian students were in their curriculum. They could be way behind, or maybe way ahead. It was hard to get an exact gauge on what kids were like on Mars. When Jordan had exchanged messages with his Educational Coordinator, she had merely said, "The Martian Development Corporation supports an enriching curriculum that will allow students to remain objective about its activities now and in the future."

Jordan stared out the window and wondered about *his* future in outer space. In the seat next to him, Leonard twitched restlessly.

"Oh, man," he said. "I really can't wait to get to Mars and get a hold of some of that crazy Mars Dust."

"Cut it out," Jordan said. "You're acting like an addict."

"I'm not an addict," Leonard said. "I just really like the stuff, that's all."

"Have you given any thought to what you're going to do when you get to Mars, Leonard?"

"I'm gonna fucking party, man!" Leonard said.

"I mean for work."

"I don't know. I'll figure it out."

Jordan looked concerned.

"Relax, Jordan," Leonard said. "I know you're nervous. It's a long trip. But you'll have me there, and Dave will be there. Don't worry. Mars is gonna be awesome."

They arrived at the spaceport, pulling into an unspectacular underground depot. Attractive women in natty red-and-white uniforms walked around handing out cups of tea and little biscuits. After an unobtrusive security scan, they approached a customs official.

"Evidence," he said.

Jordan and Leonard handed over their Devices, which she scanned.

"Reason why you're going to Mars."

"Work," Jordan said.

She waved him through.

Leonard approached.

"Reason," she said.

"Do I need one?"

"Yes. It is another planet."

"To find the answers to the party universe, sister!"

She looked Leonard up and down. "Good luck with that," she said.

They walked through the sliding doors and beheld one of the great wonders of humankind.

Humanity was at a low point, though starting to turn the corner, a little, when they'd built the Launchpad two hundred years ago. There had been a lot of false starts, explosions, and horror, but then they'd come up with the idea of reverse force, which basically allowed spaceships to fling up past the atmosphere, but softly, like dandelion fluff floating on the wind. Only after they cleared the Junk Belt would the pilots turn on the massive rocket afterburners, which could get the ship to Mars somewhere between 30 and 120 days after launch, depending on where the planets were in their orbital cycles.

The über-rockets were massive, capable of carrying two thousand people and Gaia knows how much cargo, and had been doing it successfully for two centuries. But Jordan's jaw still dropped at the sight of the SS *Obamacare*, named after the first human attempt to make sure that everyone had Enough, sitting there on the Launchpad, its recycled-alloy exterior gleaming magnificently in the warm sun of what was once called Texas before the War of Failed Secession integrated it into the rest of the world.

"Incredible," Jordan said.

"It looks like a boner with wings," said Leonard.

"You would think that."

"A huge silver boner. Like a giant space-elephant boner."

"Have some respect for science."

"What has science ever done for me?"

"Only everything."

They had this argument at least once a day. Leonard lacked commitment to principle, to ethics, to anything. Though he was intelligent—or at least Jordan *thought* he was—he was basically a walking id, as the superstitious medieval prophet Freud said, without any kind of real purpose. Maybe it was good to get him off Earth for a while.

He whirled in a circle. "Mars!" he exclaimed. "*Whoooooo*!"

The waiting room was clean but unadorned, save for posters of Mars with the MDC (Martian Development Corporation) logo. Some showed the wide-open landscapes, punctuated by happy tourists on space hikes, while other showed the ever-growing New Austin skyline. "Mars," they said. "For Now and for the Future Forever."

"Look, there's Dave!" Leonard said, waving at him. "Hey, Dave!"

Dave had come through a different entrance than Jordan and Leonard had used. He was wearing a silver lamé jacket, a bowler hat, and bright-green pants with an impossible number of zippers all over the surface. He also had a chin-beard that came down about three inches, ending in a slick, almost greasy point.

"Hey, fellow space travelers!" he said.

Leonard pointed to the beard. "Where did that come from? We just saw you two days ago."

"They sent me some Insta-Gro in my Daily Fashion Update," Dave said. "You guys really should subscribe so you don't always look so . . . Earthy."

"What's wrong with looking Earthy?" Jordan said. "By wearing approximately the same clothing, all Earth residents—"

"Oh, Jordan, spare us," Leonard said. "We're interplanetary now, right, Dave?"

"Sure," Dave said. "You bet."

"Why not have a seat with us?"

Dave looked uncomfortable, almost offended. "Oh," he said. "No. I don't wait in here. I board straight into the Executive Cabin."

"The what?"

A porter came up to Dave. "Mr. Waters, your suite is ready," he said.

"Gotta go, guys," Dave said. "I'll try to come find you in a couple of weeks. Sometimes they get lax about cabin mixing halfway through the flight."

Dave got into a hover-chair, and the porter pushed him away. Jordan was stunned. Earth had no upgrades, or cabins divided by class. People didn't need them. Everyone sat together quietly in the Levi-Trains.

"This is crazy," Jordan said.

"Ha-ha," Leonard said. "Good old Dave."

Jordan's original ticket had read "Workers' Class," for those going to Mars on a work visa, but Dave had nixed that right away, saying, "You don't want to be standing up when they put on the afterburners." He'd arranged for Jordan to be moved into Conventional, next to Leonard. They were seated in Row 112-B, Seats M and N, adjacent to the Hydration Galley, which Dave said was a must because the air can get pretty dry in space.

They boarded. Even though the rocket was massive on the outside, the interior—or at least their portion of it—felt almost like a narrow tunnel. The carpet was dirty and fraying, the seats barely big enough to hold an average human. The air smelled artificially sweet, with a certain rodent-ish undertone. Jordan and Leonard found their seats, in a row with twenty-five other seats, none of them with access to a window. There were observation decks throughout the ship, but, Jordan would soon learn, people got access to them occasionally, in large groups, unless they were seated in Executive or Platinum Executive.

Jordan fit his backpack into the overhead. They got into their seats. Jordan immediately felt his bones constrict. The seats were cold and metallic.

"We have to sit like this for a *month*?"

"They recline," Leonard said, reclining his seat about an inch. "We'll be fine."

Jordan couldn't come close to stretching out his legs. He noticed a plastic bucket underneath the seat in front of him.

"What is *this* for?"

"I don't know," Leonard said.

Leonard bounced up and down in his seat like a toddler getting ready to visit grandma. "Mars Mars Mars Mars!" he said. "Mars! Mars! Mars!"

Jordan wished he could share Leonard's enthusiasm. This felt less like a trip to Mars and more like a trip to prison. Actually, he'd been to prison recently, and this was far worse.

A voice came over the com.

"Ladies and gentleman," it said, "this is Captain Lance McBuckerton of the Martian Development Corporation. It's my pleasure to welcome you aboard the SS *Obamacare*. We're looking at an approximately six-week flight at this juncture, give or take a couple of days. The weather looks pretty good out there. We may hit a night or two of light solar winds, but those can be pretty easily avoided. For those of you who've traveled with us before, well, you know what to expect. Everyone else, please fasten your three-point harnesses and enjoy this entertaining promotional safety video. And, as always, thank you for supporting the Martian Development Corporation. See you on the other side."

The cabin lights dimmed. Holographic flight attendants appeared in the aisle, striking a pose. They gazed upward, their hands pressed in prayer, pointing up at the sky, then looked toward the crowd and said, as one: "The following presentation is the exclusive property of the Martian Development Corporation. Any rebroadcast or retransmission of this presentation without the express written consent of the MDC is punishable by six years' hard labor in the sulfur mines of Luna. Now sit back and get ready for launch."

The cabin filled with pink, purple, and light-blue laser lights as the hologrammatic flight attendants began to dance to a very light, catchy, rhythmic, inoffensive tune. They danced in and out of the aisles and over the passengers' heads. Anything is possible when you're a hologram. They sang:

We're going to Mars.
We're going to Mars.
We're going to fly right up to the stars.
We'll be hanging out
In outer space.
Mars, the special place.
Mars, the special place.
Yeah.

One of the flight attendants turned to say, "Ladies and gentlemen, you are about to undertake the great passage to the Red Planet. It's not myth anymore; it's real. But since your journey is going to cover more than 140 million miles more or less, depending on planetary orbits, there are some safety procedures you will have to follow. First, please remain tightly buckled into your safety harness at all times. If for any reason you do have to get up, whether it's to eat, use the bathroom, or gaze in wonder at the cosmos, please inform a uniformed crew member, and they will assist you from your seat."

Another one spoke: "There will be periods, sometimes lasting a day or more, where we fly through horrifying interstellar storms or come very close to the gravitational field of a comet. Do not leave your seats during any point in those disturbances, or you will surely fall and hit your head and die."

Jordan watched, horrified.

"This cabin is calibrated for Earth's gravitational field. In the event of a loss of gravity, you also must remain buckled, or you will float around and then fall, possibly to your death, when the gravitational field is restored. Also, when we lose oxygen during our flight to Mars—which will happen at least once—oxygen masks will drop from the ceiling. If our emergency oxygen supply runs out or fails, the Martian Development Corporation is not liable for any loss of life or property.

"In addition, please note the bucket in the seat in front of you. It is possible that you might require this bucket during periods of extreme turbulence. If you are coming close to filling the bucket, please ring the call button and a uniformed crew member wearing a hazmat suit will assist you."

"What in the world?" Jordan said. He looked over at Leonard, who was grinning happily. "Are you *high*?"

"As a weather balloon," Leonard said.

The fake flight attendants continued their nightmarish spiel: "Hallucinations and periods of unconsciousness might occur in the furthest reaches of space. This is normal, and do not worry, as long as your restraints are firmly in place. We've done this thousands of times. And now we encourage you to sit back, relax, and enjoy your incredible journey!"

Then they started to dance and sing again.

We're going to Mars.

We're going to Mars.

We're going to fly right up to the stars.

We're going to hang out at all the bars.

We're going to drive our very own cars.

We're going to party with our guitars.

Come to Mars with me!

Come to Mars with me!

Keep Mars Weird with me!

Yeah!

Jordan did find it weird that the slogan "Keep Mars Weird" was appearing in the safety video for an interplanetary voyage. Clearly, the MDC pushed the agenda. But Jordan was an Earthboy. He had no interest in Keeping Mars Weird.

A hologrammed screen appeared above their heads. In it, they could see the Earth, which was beginning to recede. Despite all the hysteria in the holo-presentation, this was as advertised: a lovely free-float upward. Jordan saw Austin, and the COTA track, and then, ever so gradually, the shape of the coast began to appear, from Austin all the way to the North Carolibbean. As they drifted, Jordan could see the outlines of the continents, plus the Australian archipelago created in an unfortunate early 25th century desalinization experiment. The Earth began to round into view, its clear oceans gleaming in the late-afternoon sunlight, its abundant grasslands and thriving forests generating enough breathable air so that all species could live together in harmony, that magnificent, tenderly fragile blue ball, floating alone in space. It was the Earth, and Jordan was now leaving its beloved atmosphere behind.

The starcraft floated up above the layer of space junk, which was slowly being brought down to Earth by the Moscow Magnet, but would linger for at least another two hundred years, a reminder of a less enlightened age. They drifted there for a good fifteen minutes before there came a whirring from the back of the craft. Jordan was finally feeling calm after their glorious ascent. His journey had begun, so he was going to relax, enjoy himself, and fully absorb. Jordan felt happy, and at peace with whatever future awaited.

"Ahhh," he sighed.

The engines fired, and the starship launched forward with the power of a thousand condensed suns. Jordan crushed into his seat, eyes bulging. It felt like the skin was being ripped from his face. His vision tinted gray around the edges. He could feel his skull trying to rip through the back of his head skin.

In his mind was this sound, high pitched and tinny: *Eeeeeeeeeee-eeeeeeeeee.*

And then it abated. Jordan could hear the engines' roar, and there was a feeling of heading upward, but the full acceleration appeared to have stopped. He started to doze because the oxygen supply in the cabin had been halved.

At some point, maybe an hour, maybe a day later, he heard the pilot over the com: "LUNA ROCKS!"

"Your mic is on, you idiot," another voice said.

"*Shit!*"

The cabin was eerily silent for a minute, and then the hologram appeared.

"Ladies and gentlemen," the hologram said, "we're entering a lunar-construction debris field from Luna. Please hold tight."

The ship chicaned right. Jordan's brains and eyeballs went in the opposite direction. It swerved left. Then back right again, and then it sloped downward sharply before whooshing upward. Jordan felt dizzy. No, he was dying, No, he was going to be—

He reached for the bucket in front of him and got it to his face just in time.

"*Bleargh!*" He emptied the contents of his stomach into the bucket. He looked up, the ship chicaned again, and he vomited afresh.

"Gaia help me!" Jordan moaned. He looked around. Hundreds of other people were upchucking violently at once, heaving desperately, screaming. Their heads shook, and their insides emptied. The walls and aisles of the plane were awash in splatter. The cabin filled with the stink of barf and bile, which made Jordan vomit even harder. Next to him, Leonard continued to grin happily.

"This is awesome!" Leonard said. "Like a great space coaster!"

"How—" Jordan said, before retching deeply and bleatingly into the bucket again.

"It's all good," said Leonard. "I made Space Cakes. Lots of them. Do you want one?"

"No," Jordan said queasily. "It makes me tired . . ."

The ship swooped downward again. Something struck its hull. Jordan could smell smoke.

"Junk asteroids!" the captain screamed into the com. "Thousands of them! Evasive maneuvers! Mayday!"

The ship was being battered from all sides. Jordan leaned over the bucket and gave a low moan—"*Roooooooooooooooooo*"—as he retched up a brownish liquid that was never meant to leave his body.

Three rows in front of them, a man, panicked, unbuckled himself, screaming, "Get me off this ship!"

The man floated upward. The rocket jerked to the left, then right, then left again. The man crashed against the hull with each jerk. His neck cracked instantly after the first, and when it was over he lolled there above them, tongue out. The cabin filled with howls.

Jordan looked at Leonard, put his hand out, and said, "I'll take two."

7

The next few weeks passed regrettably. Jordan and Leonard sat upright on their straight-backed benches, with very little to keep them occupied. Jordan tried to amuse himself by remembering the words to every Vincent St. Aubrey D'Shea poem, but that grew stale after a while. He found himself nodding away for long stretches—hours, maybe even days. The flight attendants would periodically pass out little clear pills, which clouded his mind and his vision. Every time he snapped back to awareness, Leonard was sitting there grinning, playing holographic poker with a Mangapus avatar.

One morning—or afternoon, or evening; time had lost all distinction to him aboard this space tube, where the view outside was black and empty and the view inside was purple neon and emptier still—Jordan awoke with a start. His buttock bones were burning, but he couldn't stand up. They only let passengers stretch in groups of twenty, at intermittent schedules, or else the aisles would be totally crammed at all times. He reached into his pack, hoping to tap into the stash. But he found only crumbs.

"Sonofabitch!" he exclaimed.

"Huh?" Leonard said.

"We're out of special cake."

"Oh."

"What am I going to do?"

"I don't know," Leonard said. "Sometimes it's good to take a break."

"That is not an option," Jordan said.

Jordan's eyes felt raw. And he smelled like a cheese factory in a power outage. This flight had gone on forever, and there was no remediation for his ills except for Space Cakes. He pressed his flight-attendant call button frantically. A groggy attendant approached.

"You again," he said. "What?"

"Hey," Jordan said. "My friend and I are out of special cake."

"So?"

"So can we buy some?"

"Of course you can."

"Great."

"In Executive Class or above."

"Just give Executive Class a ring for us, then, would you?"

"Oh no," the attendant said. "You have to *be* Executive Class."

"Not for marijuana," Jordan said. "It's in the Global Constitution. It's for the people. It's from the Earth."

"The Global Constitution only applies on the globe."

"But—"

"Sorry, sir. We don't sell those up here."

"But I *need* it. This is *unjust*!"

Jordan had deeply cared about injustice back home. Then again, he'd never experienced much of it. No one had. That was part of the new human promise, that everyone would have Enough of what they wanted, but not too much. Denying a beloved resource because of scarcity, well, that was in his frame of reference. But denying it because it was being reserved for someone else, someone *better*, well, that just didn't compute.

Jordan unbuckled his belt and stood. "*Please*," he said. "Please can I have some special cakes?"

"Sir, you have to sit down," the attendant said.

"Seriously, dude," Leonard said. "Relax. I'm sorry I ever gave you some in the first place."

"I will *not* relax," Jordan said. "I want my cakes. This is *hell*!"

"Sir, if you'd just take the clear pills—"

"I don't need your soporifics! I want the ganja gift of Gaia in my mouth right now so I can relax in this terrifying metal tube that is *eating my brain*."

"Oh no," Leonard said. "Space madness. There's a Mangapus episode about this."

Jordan always had been highly sensitive, mentally and emotionally. He could snap. Certainly, it seemed like he was snapping now. That's why it was dangerous for him to ingest THC. It calmed his brain. Or he could be a maniac.

The attendant spoke into his wrist: "Incipient space madness in row 112-B," he said. "Restraining devices may be required."

"Madness?" Jordan said. "*Madness?* That is ridiculous. I just want *drugs and I want them now*!"

"I have drugs. There are clear pills. And you'll sleep for days."

"I don't want to sleep," Jordan moaned. "Don't you understand? People are dying in here, and I don't want to be one of them."

During the initial asteroid storm, two more passengers had died: a woman whose neck restraint was improperly aligned had ended up with a snapped spine, and a man had choked to death on his own vomit. Since then, two elderly people had passed, their constitutions simply unable to bear the rigors of interplanetary flight. They had all signed ironclad waivers, so the MDC wasn't liable. Depending on the prices of their tickets, their bodies had either been placed into cryogenic storage, to be shipped home to family on the next available return shuttle to Earth, or, less ceremoniously, dumped out a secure airlock along with approximately two tons of frozen fecal matter and assorted garbage.

"Sir," the flight attendant, said, "we've lost five people on this flight. Out of more than three thousand passengers. Do you know how many people died on the first manned flight to Mars?"

"Not exactly," Jordan said. Maybe in a calmer moment, he would have remembered. But this wasn't a calmer moment.

"Five. Out of seven astronauts. And do you know how many people died on the first *commercial* flight to Mars?"

"Um, five?"

"More like fifty-five. Out of a hundred and twenty. And *thousands* of people have died in the last century trying to get to Mars. Why? Because it's another planet. It is millions of miles away. The journey is long and tough and fraught with perils that Earth people can barely begin to imagine. This flight may not seem like much to you, but it has been very carefully engineered to vastly increase the odds that you will get to your destination alive. So you'll forgive me if I don't have a lot of sympathy that you're out of your special marijuana cakes."

"I *demand—*"

"No, sir. I demand that you shut the fuck up right now, or I will inject you full of Morphinerol, enough to sedate you for the remaining weeks or months or however the hell long it takes to get your sorry, spoiled ass to Mars, at which point you'll be someone else's problem."

From behind him, Jordan heard, "Is someone making trouble again?"

He looked up. It was Dave Waters. He was wearing a gold jumpsuit, studded with felt-blue stars, and a bowler hat.

"My *man*," said Leonard.

"Where have *you* been?" Jordan said.

"Just partyin' in Executive," Dave said. "Sorry I couldn't get here sooner. Things got a little crazy."

Jordan tried to adopt a casual stance. "That's cool," he said. "I like your outfit."

"I call them my space pajamas," Dave said. "What's going on here?"

Jordan pointed at the attendant. "This person here is trying to pump me full of Morphinerol."

"That's pretty heavy," Dave said.

"What we *want*," Jordan said, "is Space Cakes. We ran out, and I'm starting to feel a little claustrophobic."

"He's going loopy cuckoo," Leonard clarified.

"We've got plenty of Space Cakes up in Executive," said Dave. "*So* many."

"Well, that's good for you," said Jordan. "But it doesn't help us much."

"Sure it does." Dave pulled two large purple tickets out of his gold lamé jumpsuit. "VIP, baby!"

"Nice!" said Leonard.

"For how long?" Jordan said.

"Rest of the trip, man, however long that is."

Jordan exhaled. "Thank Gaia."

Dave gave Jordan a sniff. "You need to shower first, though," he said. "You smell like shit."

"We don't have showers up here."

"*What?* I had no clue. I totally would have come for you guys earlier. No worries. I have a full tub with jets in my suite."

"Your suite?"

"Suites for the sweet!" said Leonard.

"Let's jam, broham," said Dave.

Jordan got his bag from the overhead. The attendant looked at him with disdain.

"You got lucky," the attendant said.

"I got what I deserved," said Jordan.

"You haven't even *begun* to get what you deserve," the attendant mumbled. He walked away. The buzzer was going off. Somewhere on the ship, someone had an *actual* problem.

♦ ♦ ♦

They went up a set of winding stairs, through another wretched-smelling economy cabin, down another set of stairs and through another cabin, which ended with a set of sliding glass doors.

Executive security guards were waiting for them there. Dave gave one of them a little nod.

"Everything OK, sir?" he said.

"Sound the bells," Dave said. "We're home."

Dave waved his right hand twice to the left, and then in a circle, and then back to the right. The doors whooshed open, and then the whole room moved upward.

"This ship has elevators?" Leonard said.

"Hiding in plain sight," said Dave.

They went up two levels, and then walked through another cabin, this one small and full of children—a kind of seventh level of travel hell. The children were running around and screaming, unsupervised, doing everything short of flinging poop, though that probably wasn't uncommon, either.

There was a second set of glass doors, a second whoosh, an elevator ride down, and finally they emerged into a sort of lobby. Smooth music played, and lush orchids decorated a circular desk, behind which sat two women in neat one-piece uniforms that bore the MDC logo. There was a placard that read, in white letters on black, "THE EXECUTIVE EXPERIENCE."

"Welcome back, Mr. Waters," said one of them.

"Yolo," Dave said.

"Are these your guests?"

"Yep, Kincaid and Tolliver. Twin testicles of Terra."

"That's nice."

"They'll be with me for the duration," Dave said.

"Of course."

"'Twin testicles of Terra,'" Leonard said, chucking Dave on the shoulder. "You're an ass."

Dave whooshed his hand in a circle. The doors opened. They stepped into a vestibule, walls lined with fine leather. The carpet was thick and deep under their feet. The air smelled like lavender.

The vestibule spun around.

Jordan and Leonard beheld paradise.

It was a space similar in size to the one where Jordan and Leonard had been. The similarities ended there. Rather than three hundred people crammed onto benches, the men and women of Executive—thirty of them at most—sprawled about on body-length sofas, sipping cocktails, popping pieces of fruit and little squares of meat into their mouths. The conversation was low, the ambience dark and misty. It was an older crowd, their tasteful clothes rustling like gentle breezes. A three-piece band played a popular tune, in the style of old lounge jazz.

We have passed our moon.

We have passed the stars.

It makes me want to croon.

I'm going home to Mars . . .

"Whoa," Leonard said.

Everyone was wearing the shiniest outfits and the finest fashion. They were fabulous rich peacocks, all of them. In fact, one woman walked by wearing a headdress made of peacock feathers, which Jordan, and even Leonard, found shocking.

"I can't believe it," Jordan said.

"I know," said Dave. "Wild, right?"

"It's against the law to wear animal."

"Money talks," said Dave. "Poverty walks. You like?"

What wasn't to like? Everything in the room was first rate, from the lighting fixtures to the flooring to the floor-to-ceiling, six-paned windows that allowed the passengers to look over outer space like the lords and ladies of the Milky Way they were. Jordan was stunned. Even regional representatives to the Earth Council didn't live this way. Even his *mother* didn't live like this. But he was especially stunned because, he realized, he liked it. Even wanted it.

A relaxed-looking waiter, wearing a freshly pressed tuxedo, walked up holding a tray. "Can I get you guys a drink?" he said, and then, crinkling his nose, "And maybe a *shower*?"

"Give them a break," said Dave. "They've been in steerage."

"Do you have . . . do you have . . . freshly squeezed apple juice?" Jordan asked.

"Of course we do!"

"And a Space Cake."

"Medium or extra strength?"

"Medium," said Leonard.

"Extra," said Jordan.

"Extra, then," said Leonard. "You have any Kentucky bourbon?"

"From a casket dating to the Civil War," said the waiter.

"Wow," said Leonard. "All the way back to 2175."

"No, not the Pan-Eurasian Civil War. The *American* Civil War."

"Wow," said Leonard.

From behind him, Jordan heard, "And who are these two scrubby-looking characters, David?"

Jordan turned around. A broad-shouldered, gray-haired man, dressed austerely but very expensively, filled the space behind him, and then some.

"Hey, Dad!" Dave said. "These are some old school buddies of mine. You remember them. Leonard and Jordan."

"Of course," said the elder Waters, making it very clear with his indifferent expression that he didn't remember either of them. There was a brief, uncomfortable pause. Then he said, "How do you boys like my little starship here?"

"*Your* ship?" Leonard said.

"Dad is the head of the MDC now," said Dave. "That's how I got your VIP passes."

"We like it great now that we're in Executive," Leonard said. "Please don't make us leave!"

Dick Waters gave a laugh that seemed sincere but almost certainly wasn't. He slapped Leonard on the back. "Behave yourself and you can stay," he said. "What are your plans for Mars?"

"I just thought I'd cruise around," Leonard said. "Check things out. Maybe do some writing."

Waters narrowed his eyes. "Uh-huh," he said.

"It's going to be fun," Leonard said. "And exciting."

"Well, I'm not going to Mars to party," Jordan said. "I got a teaching job."

"*Teaching?*" Waters said. "That's a funny one."

"What's wrong with teaching?"

"Nothing at all," Waters said. "As long as you teach the right things. And now, if you'll excuse me . . ."

Dick Waters wandered off to some dark corner to speak softly to an unimaginably wealthy Martian widow in a low voice.

"Oh, he *liked* you," Dave Waters said.

"Really?" Jordan said.

"Definitely. He won't even talk to most of my friends."

The waiter brought their refreshments. Jordan sipped on his apple juice. It was more delicious than anything he'd ever tasted. Then he popped the Space Cake in his mouth, and *that* took the prize.

"Is this *organic* cannabutter?" Jordan said.

"Our cows only eat pure Uruguayan hybrid grass.".

"Wow."

"Can I get you anything else, sir?"

"Not right now."

The waiter slid Jordan a bill.

Jordan looked at it, then looked at it again. "Twenty-four thousand credits!"

Leonard spit out a mouthful of seven-century-old bourbon.

"I don't have that kind of money," Jordan said.

"Don't worry," said Dave. "I got it." He turned to the waiter. "Put it on my tab."

"Of course, Mr. Waters."

"Man, talk about knowing the right people," said Leonard.

"Next time, get the regular bourbon, dude," Dave said.

"I'm really sorry," said Leonard.

"Naw, I'm just fucking with you," said Dave. "I have unlimited money. Are you guys ready to get going?"

"Going where?" said Leonard.

"This is just the forward lounge," Dave said.

"We are in the *life*!" Leonard said.

Jordan felt the Space Cake begin to take effect. His brain was lightening, and so was his mood. His nerves were calming, the madness receding. But even though he felt relaxed, he was a little more skeptical than Leonard. Everyone was equal. They should only have Enough and no more.

But even he had to admit that it was pretty nice down here in Executive.

8

Jordan stepped out of the shower and rubbed the thick white cotton towel all over his body. He'd been in there for fifteen minutes, at least, shampooing and conditioning twice. As Space Cake users had known for centuries, he'd discovered that there are few things more pleasurable than a high shower.

The bathroom was marble and glass. A six-paned window, with an automatic retractable screen to guard against solar flares, sat next to a two-person jet tub, overlooking the universe. Jordan turned to the wall-length mirror to take his measure. His eyes were still red rimmed and his space-beard still patchy. He hadn't been able to find a razor. But his skin felt fresh and untroubled. In steerage, they'd passed out one vaguely warm moist cloth every twenty-four hours, and you were forced to mop yourself with that. The cabin had smelled like an abandoned farm.

There was a silver tunic hanging next to the shower. Jordan slipped it on. It looked faintly ridiculous. Dave had given it to him, saying that's what everyone was wearing this week.

Jordan walked into the bedroom, which was unoccupied. Dave had three rooms on the starship, all to himself. His entire suite was about the size of Jordan and Leonard's apartment back on Earth.

Dave and Leonard were in the living room. As the wonders of the universe spread before them in a panoramic window view, they were busy playing holographic laser tennis.

"*Ace!*" Leonard shouted.

Dave looked up. "Aren't you the hip thing?" he said. "Very of the moment."

"How do you know what's in fashion right now?" Jordan said. "You've been up in this thing for weeks."

"Are you kidding?" Dave said. "The starship *sets* the trends."

"I feel like I'm getting ready to go to an asexual Roman space disco."

"That can be arranged," Dave said.

The doors to his suite whooshed open. In walked a young woman wearing the same tunic as Jordan. But she wore it a lot better. She was one cool drink of space juice. Her dark hair poured down the back of her neck, draping across her shoulders like a cat luxuriating on its favorite chair. She puckered her lips, touched with the precise shade of silver gloss to match her tunic. That was the only makeup she wore on her perfect nut-brown face.

"Are you boys in here doing boy things again?" she said. "So glad to see the Three Compañeros together again."

"Jordan, Leonard," Dave said, "you guys remember my sister, Crystal."

"Howdy," Leonard said.

Jordan remembered Crystal Waters. She'd been a spunky preteen girl the last time he'd seen her—lots of fun, very bright, full of promise. But that had been a long time ago. The promise had more than been fulfilled.

To Jordan, Crystal Waters was a vision of almost unimaginably confident loveliness, surrounded by a corona of light. All thoughts of his formerly dear Daril evaporated like so much stardust. His unwanted trip to Mars had been immutably transformed into a cosmic quest for love.

"Crystal?" Jordan croaked.

"That is me," Crystal said.

"You . . . you're perfect!"

"Perfectly thirsty," she said. "I haven't had a drink in nearly two hours. Why don't you nerds wrap up your tennis match and come dancing with me?"

"Dancing in space!" Leonard exclaimed. "Rad!"

"This one's excitable, Dave," she said. "We'll have to get him a leash."

"Oh, Leonard's OK."

Crystal looked Jordan up and down. "Did I miss the memo about Dress Like David Bowie Spartacus Day?"

Jordan stammered, "It's . . . it's the same thing you're wearing."

"Everything looks better on a woman," she said.

"She's got you there," Leonard said.

Oh, she had him, all right.

They walked down a long, neon-lit hallway filled with the thumping of electronic music. Jordan couldn't believe it. There was no way to tell this even existed from the outside. They passed a sign that read, simply, "Party Zone."

"I didn't know the Mars shuttle had a Party Zone," Jordan said.

"We don't advertise," said Dave. "Invite only. Keeps out the riffraff."

"Oh, don't be such a snob, David," Crystal said. "Sometimes I think we should have more riffraff around here. Isn't that right, Jordan?"

"What?" Jordan said. "Oh yes, everyone should be equal."

"That is adorable," said Crystal. "*You* are adorable."

Dave and Leonard ran on ahead. "*Whoooo*!" they shouted. "Party Zone!"

Crystal took Jordan's hand, as naturally as though they'd been together for years. Jordan started to sweat. His heart shredded. He felt a swelling down below. What was her game? Jordan didn't even care. He was in love for the second time in his life.

"So, Jordan," Crystal said, "how long do you plan to stay on Mars?"

"I don't know," he said. "It depends on my sentence."

"Sentence? What do you mean?"

"Well, it's kind of embarrassing."

"You can tell me, Jordan," she said. "We're old friends. You can tell me *anything*."

"OK," Jordan said. "Back on Earth, I got into some trouble."

"You don't *look* like trouble."

"I'm not. But there was this girl."

"There usually is."

"And I really liked her a lot. Anyway, one night Leonard and Dave and I went out for ramen and I saw her there with another guy. I went completely nuts. I wanted to kill him."

"And *did* you?"

"No."

"Oh," she said, "that's a shame. He deserved it for taking your girl away from you."

"Are you teasing me?"

"Not at all. It's very romantic. We all need to fight for what we love."

She was wonderful.

"There was a fight, though," Jordan said. "So I got transferred to Mars instead of going to jail. I have to admit I'm not happy. I love the Earth."

"Please, sweetie," she said. "The Earth is *boring*. It hasn't had any action at all in two hundred years."

"Well, I love it."

"When you get to Mars, you'll see what I mean."

"I don't intend to get any action on Mars. I'm just going to teach the children and serve the community."

"You're a teacher?"

"Yes," he said proudly.

"That is *adorable.* We'll be able to spend a lot of time together, then."

"That'd be nice," Jordan said. "But teaching is a very demanding job."

"Not on Mars, it's not."

"I intend to—"

"Just follow the script," she said. "Not like you have any choice."

Crystal stopped in front of what looked like a blank section of hull. She knocked four times. A panel opened in the top of the door. Jordan could see a pair of eyes peeping out.

"What?" said a voice attached to the eyes.

"The dust is here," Crystal said.

On a typical evening, Jordan preferred a nice bowl of fried rice followed by a motivational concert and then home for historical study and bed. He wasn't going to get that here. A full door opened where the panel had been. Maybe forty people, all young and staggeringly beautiful and dressed very fashionably in top hats and monocles and corncob pipes and reprints of vintage twenty-second-century T-shirts, danced in the center of the room to an obnoxious rhythm. One woman wore a one-piece dress that depicted a beach when she shimmied in one direction and waves when she swayed in another. Actually, that piece of clothing was kind of cool, Jordan admitted. But the guy she was dancing with, who wore a metal birdcage containing a live parrot on his head, sort of canceled her out.

"Jordan!" Crystal shouted. "I want to introduce you to my friends!" She started pointing around the room. "That's Abagail, that's Abilene, Fiona, Marcus, Cole, Kole, Coal, Kip, Lemongrass, LaGuardia . . ."

Leonard and David came dancing up. Leonard was wearing a funky green wizard's hat and appeared to already be extremely drunk.

"You got the dust?" Dave asked his sister.

"Of course I do, darling," she said. "It's extra-premium grade."

"Hey, everyone!" Dave shouted. "Crystal's got the dust!"

"And it's only six million a sack!" Crystal said.

That insane price didn't seem to bother the young travelers in the Party Zone though. Crystal produced a Scan-Watch. The people entered chip-credits. They took their little velvet bags of Mars Dust and emptied out the powder onto tables, snorting it in great, greedy gulps. The air filled with a gleeful whooping, and the music got louder as the rocket hurtled ever nearer to Mars, the most awesome party place in the whole entire universe.

"What about you, Jordan?" said Crystal, her eyes wide as baseballs. She was sniffling after a particularly heady dose of the dust. "Care for a snoot?"

"I'm sorry," Jordan said. "That's not in my budget."

"Silly," she said, swatting at him. "You don't have to pay! You're a friend of the family."

Dave and Leonard came bouncing up. "Come on, buddy," Leonard said.

"I don't—"

"Why not just once? We're gonna be up in this can for at least a couple more weeks."

"Really—"

"Tell you what," Crystal said. She leaned into Jordan and told him just what she'd do if he sampled some of her dust. It was the kind of offer rarely made on Earth, on Mars, or anywhere in the cosmos.

"Well," he said. "Maybe just one bag."

"There you go," she said.

Crystal handed him the bag. He moved to go spread it on a glass table.

"Don't bother with the show," she said. "Just stick your nose straight in and snort."

He did as she said. For a second, it felt like someone had lit up his nostrils with a flamethrower. Then those flames hit his brain and he was gone, whooshing through his mind at a million miles an hour. Every joint, every cell tingled in instant ecstasy.

Dave, Leonard, and Crystal were jumping up and down. "Mars!" they shouted. "Mars Mars Mars Mars Mars!"

Jordan never wanted to feel another way ever again. Crystal leaned toward him and licked his ear, like a predatory she-lion. He started jumping, too.

"Mars Mars Mars Mars Mars Mars Mars!"

9

Jordan awoke with a shudder. The cabin was rattling about. He felt like a gambling die inside a cup.

Where am I?

He really couldn't remember.

His head appeared to be at the end of a king-sized bed. The sheets were strewn wildly about. As his eyes focused, he could see that the cabin had been reduced to a riotous, chaotic mess of clothes and empty bottles and random bits of detritus. Also, he was naked.

At the other end of the bed, Crystal hugged a pillow as though it were some kind of precious doll. She looked calm and secure, like the queen of a peaceable realm.

Jordan got out of bed. He farted. Everything felt dank and foggy. He staggered unsteadily to the bathroom. The door was only a few feet away. There was a thunking sound, and the entire cabin lurched to the left. Jordan stumbled but caught himself on the doorframe. Over it appeared, in green neon letters, the words, "Executive Class: Proceed with Caution."

In the vast, marbled bathroom, Jordan flipped on the light. He looked nightmarish. His eyes were rimmed with red canals; his face, which he normally kept baby-clear, was as stubbly as a wheat field after harvest. His lips were crusted with old drool, his belly with something far more unmentionable. He was a mess.

Great Gaia, what had he been doing? How long had he been doing it? Where was he? Who was he? Why?

As if to answer his vast existential crisis, an automatic shade, positioned next to the two-person jetted bathtub, drew up with a soothing whir, revealing a floor-to-ceiling window. There it sat, a great dusty-red bauble, floating clearly in space like a half-forgotten dream.

Mars.

Jordan suddenly knew his purpose. He understood. Soon, he would become one of the first ten million people to ever set foot on the Red Planet. He was a cosmic pioneer, if not of the first order, then at least of the tenth, and that was enough.

Crystal appeared by his side, naked, perfect. "Isn't it unbelievable?" she said.

"It truly is," said Jordan.

"This is my fifth time," she said, "and every time is like the first."

"I've never seen something so beautiful."

She pointed toward the planet. "There aren't any oceans," she said. "We've looked. We even dug a little, once. A thousand people got swallowed into a sand pit. That was unfortunate. But it *looks* like there are oceans. You can see them, there."

There were lighter shapes that looked like continents. Jordan knew intellectually that this was a planet, and that it had probably once looked a lot like Earth, but now he *felt* it, quite deeply, and he became sentimental.

"Jordan," Crystal said. "Are those *tears* welling up in your eyes?"

"Maybe a little," Jordan said. "It's just so beautiful."

She placed a hand on his cock and began to stroke gently.

"W-what are you doing?"

"I wanted to give you a little Martian memory."

It began to come back to him now. Time had been lost in a vast molten orgy of drugs. The Mars Dust not only filled his brain with an unimaginable ecstasy, but it also engorged his penis terrifically, filling him with insatiable lust. He had a vision, vague but very real, of riding Crystal like a pony, slapping her magnificent ass while she screamed his name. How many times he'd done this, he didn't quite know. It was unclear if he'd eaten, or bathed, or anything else.

"We have less than half a day before they turn on the thrusters," Crystal said. "We should do some dust."

"I kind of want to keep my head clear . . ."

Crystal held out her right hand. There was a little velvet bag of dust in it. Where it had come from, Jordan couldn't be sure. She was very naked, and there'd been nowhere to hide it.

"Just a little," she said. "To wake us up. We can share."

"I don't know . . ."

Crystal pouted. "I guess the last two weeks don't mean anything to you, then," she said.

"What? No, not at all," said Jordan. "I just—"

"I could have fucked anyone on this spaceship," she said. "Anyone I wanted. Of any subgender. Because my daddy owns it. He owns everything. He owns all of you. But I chose Jordan Kincaid. And why?"

She tightened her grip a bit and gave his boner a little pump. Jordan gulped.

"Because you're gorgeous," she said, "*and* cute. And also a little naïve. At least you *were* naïve. Mars needs men like you, men who are smart and idealistic and hot. I'm tired of the same old people without ideas, people who just want to party. We need people who are going to move Mars forward. Are you going to move Mars forward, Jordan Kincaid?"

She moved forward on his dick, with a rhythmic stroking motion. Jordan turned his head and saw the Red Planet looming, rife with hedonistic possibility.

"Yes," he said.

"That's right," she said. "Now stop whining and snort some of this dust off my tits."

This was not the Martian entry Jordan Kincaid had expected. But his mother had told him to enjoy his adventure, and Gaia knew he was enjoying himself. Everybody should have Enough. He believed that fully. But maybe it was OK if some people—not too many—went a little bit beyond their quota. As the self-styled princess of Mars sprinkled the highest-quality-possible brand of space drugs on her perfect tits, guiding his head toward them while simultaneously pumping his penis, he thought, *I can never have Enough of* this.

♦ ♦ ♦

Ten hours later, after Jordan and Crystal had taken two bubble baths, and Crystal had her family barber come in and give Jordan a shave and haircut and manicure and exfoliating scrub and hot Martian rock massage and steam-rain shower aromajet therapy, after Jordan and Crystal had enjoyed a sumptuous brunch of three-hundred-year-old fried Virginia ham and endangered Martian goose egg omelet, and Jordan and Crystal had made sweet love three times under the ever-reddening sky, it was over. There was a knock at the door of Crystal's suite. Jordan opened it, wearing a complimentary velour bathrobe.

There stood a flight attendant, looking harried.

"Mr. Kincaid," he said.

"Yes?" Jordan said.

"I'm here to take you back to your seat."

"My seat?"

"Yes, we're landing in ten hours, and everyone has to be in their assigned seat when we land."

"But why can't I just stay here? There are plenty of seats."

He looked back at Crystal. She shrugged.

"It's protocol," he said. "Executives disembark at least an hour earlier than regular passengers. Sometimes more, if there are problems with transit papers. If they take their guests with them, it causes confusion."

"But . . ."

Jordan didn't want to leave Crystal. She was his everything, and he was, as she called him, her "mighty tit-slave." It was hard for him to imagine that just two months earlier, he was nearly engaged to Daril. She seemed so provincial to him now, compared with what Crystal had to offer, which was, apparently, everything. Without her, he would be dried up, antiquated, nothing.

"We'll catch up later," she said.

"How?"

"Don't worry," she said. "We'll see each other again."

After luxuriating forever in the complimentary robes of Executive—or naked, in satin sheets—Jordan's Earth unitard felt constricting and itchy. The attendant walked him down the hall, far too quickly. Jordan ran his hands over the leather-lined Executive walls as though he'd never feel anything like them again.

Leonard sprawled in the hall, snoring happily. The attendant nudged him with his foot.

"Mr. Tolliver," he said.

"Mommy," Leonard said.

"Time to go."

"Mmmmm," Leonard said.

"I left him here five minutes ago," the exasperated attendant said to Jordan.

Leonard sat up. "Oh, hey, Jordan."

"Hey, Leonard."

"Did you have a good time?"

"Yes," Jordan said.

"Me, too," Leonard said. "I had the best time. The good times will never end."

Leonard, who was usually wrong, had never been more wrong about anything.

10

The smell got worse and worse as the attendant led a staggering Jordan and Leonard back toward their assigned seats. It stank of rancid meat and wet wool. He remembered his trips to the Rocky Mountain Free Zone, how he'd stood atop Mount Obama, breathing the sweet air of free humanity. This was the opposite smell, in every way.

"Two more people died while you jokers were gone," the attendant said.

"Oh yeah?" said Leonard.

"That's *still* a good percentage."

"OK."

"One guy had a blood vessel explode in his brain. It happens. Someone else choked. That's what you get when you ask for free celery."

"Right."

A guy was sprawled across their seats, sleeping angrily, like a hobo at a twentieth-century bus stop. The attendant nudged him. But the guy didn't budge. He nudged him again. Nothing.

"Come on, buddy," he said.

Finally, after a couple of minutes of this, the attendant tumbled him off. The guy hit the ground and woke with a start.

"What the hell?" he said.

"These assholes are back from their Executive vacation."

"Freakin' MDC fascists," the guy said. His beard nearly touched his chest. He looked near death. Jordan was fuzzy in the brain, but his skin looked clear and fresh. As he looked around the cabin, he noticed the rest of the travelers seemed exhausted and pallid, subhuman.

"Sit down and buckle in," the attendant said. "And *don't* make any trouble."

Jordan and Leonard sat on their benches and strapped into their harnesses, like they were on some sort of budget carnival ride. It had been a lot better in Executive. Leonard reached into his bag and pulled out a couple of cookies. He handed one to Jordan.

"These should last us until we land," he said.

"I hope so," Jordan said as he scarfed it down eagerly. He didn't know the difference between being high and not being high anymore.

The lights went out. A giant hologram of Mars appeared in the center of the cabin.

"Ladies and gentlemen," said a disembodied voice, "we have now begun our final descent to Mars, the Red Planet. You'll be in landing in New Austin, home to the headquarters of the Martian Development Corporation. To tell you more about your destination, here's Richard Waters, founder and CEO of the MDC."

The image of Mars disappeared, replaced by a full-body hologram of Dave's dad, whom Jordan and Leonard had seen in the flesh not too many days before. He was wearing a suit, and appeared in an open office space, surrounded by eager-looking workers, all of them doing very important things at their desk, backed by floor-to-ceiling windows overlooking a vast Martian desert.

"Hi, I'm Dick Waters," he said.

Leonard laughed. "Dick," he said. "Waters."

"And I'm pleased to welcome you all to New Austin, the flagship city of the Martian Development Corporation. New Austin is a city unique in the universe, with our galaxy-class live music scene, award-winning restaurants, and thousands of independent businesses that serve the liveliest and most unique professional clientele for millions of miles. We have unparalleled access to hiking and all the great natural activities that Mars has to offer. I consider it a great privilege to stand at a desk every day overlooking Martian Springs, a naturally occurring phenomenon that the MDC created by tapping into a unique groundwater source seven hundred and fifty miles below the surface of New Austin, which now provides recreation and fishing opportunities to thousands of New Austin residents every year. It's one of the many ways that MDC is helping to Keep Mars Weird."

Waters started walking as he talked, making it appear that he was moving down the aisle toward Jordan and Leonard. His hologram moved past them and then pivoted and turned back around.

"'Now then, Dick'"—Leonard laughed again—"you might ask, 'What does "Keep Mars Weird" actually mean? Do I *have* to be weird to live on Mars?' Of course not. Most of the residents of New Austin are completely normal, in every way. At least on the surface. But weirdness is a state of mind. It means that at MDC, we're committed to maintaining Mars's unique cultural identity, to ensure that every man, woman, and child has the opportunity to express themselves how they want, when they want, and where they want, to give them the unique freedoms that are their birthright. Keeping Mars Weird is more than a slogan, or a motto, and it's far from an empty promise. It is the absolute lifeblood of what makes Mars such a great place to live, work, and play. You can shop at our many boutiques and eat at our hundreds of galaxy-class restaurants. I think you'll agree that there's no place like Mars. Now please follow your flight attendants' instructions, and get ready for the adventure of a lifetime. Welcome to Mars. And remember . . ."

Everyone in the hologrammed office, dozens of people, turned to face front, and they all said at once, "KEEP MARS WEIRD!"

Jordan didn't even know what to think anymore. His trip to Mars had certainly been weird thus far, though maybe not in the way that Dick Waters had intended. It was strange to think that his father had made this same voyage more than twenty years before. What had it been like then? Why had he come home so suddenly? What had forced his hand? More importantly, what was Jordan's love, Crystal, doing right now? Was she luxuriating in her bathtub, rubbing a warm, oil-soaked washcloth all over her delicious mocha skin?

Jordan felt an all too familiar tumescence growing in his pants. No. He needed to focus. The drugs had been fun, and the sex, what vague bits of it he could remember, had been *really* fun, but it was all over now. He was going to Mars, and he was going to teach, and he was going to make sure that everyone on the planet knew that it was OK to be equal, and to have Enough.

The cabin filled with the MDC logo, superimposed onto the face of Mars, flashing, over and over again, as the theme song played:

We're going to Mars.

We're going to Mars.

We're going to fly right up to the stars.

Leonard stared ahead, grinning. The rest of the passengers looked waxy, a lot less concerned with keeping Mars weird than just surviving the night. Once they arrived, they'd be so grateful to be alive that they'd do anything the MDC wanted. They would be willing cogs in a machine that they could in no way, nor did they have any desire to, comprehend. Any excitement had been deposited millions of miles ago. Now they just wanted out of their cage.

The video shut off suddenly; the lights went out; the cabin started to rattle. Again people were screaming. Jordan felt himself pressed back in the seat. He couldn't breathe. Again it felt like his face was peeling off. He wondered if they were having these problems in Executive, or if there was some kind of extra shield from the fact that they were about to violently penetrate a space vacuum.

"Ladies and gentlemen, prepare for atmospheric entry," a panicked voice said over the sound system.

"Shit, shit, shiiiiiiiiiiiit!" said another as the cabin began to rattle violently. "Here we go!"

Three hours, two radiation-drenched dust storms, and seven violent deaths later, the great dome opened, and the MDC ship floated down onto the New Austin spaceport. The totals: fourteen dead, twenty-two irreversibly brain damaged, sixty-five lives shortened due to decreased heart and lung capacity. Only a handful of those would be granted a full refund after a drawn-out procedure with the MDC's vast team of lawyers. In Executive, passengers had eaten a record number of 14,672 sustainably farmed prawns. It was one of the most successful flights in MDC history.

All about the cabin, people were standing, stretching, and gasping with relief. They had survived and were ready to start their new lives, or at least their vacations, on Mars.

The planet couldn't wait to take their money.

11

The good passengers in Executive had been precleared, most of them with Extreme Exemptions, so they were able to take their time packing up after the ship docked on Mars. Some of them even enjoyed rain showers or one last cocktail in the lounge before stepping into a private shuttle that would take them to their luggage. After a quick, friendly stamp of their Star Papers, they headed off to whatever transport they'd arranged. There was no waiting. Executives never waited for anything.

Jordan and Leonard, on the other hand, stood in the aisle of the starship for forty-five minutes, stench emanating from the floors and the walls and the rear galleys. It smelled like they were swimming at the bottom of a compost hole. Jordan had a bellyful of rich food, and Gaia knows what else he'd put into his body. He gagged several times but somehow held it in.

Finally, someone opened a door somewhere, and the passengers began to trudge off. They'd been stuck in this compartment for weeks, an atmosphere about as lively and healthy as a storage locker. Most of them couldn't even remember why they'd decided to go to Mars in the first place. The Martian solar day is actually fairly close to the length of the Earth day, but the solar year is nearly twice as long. This led to a jet lag so immense that people often had to spend their first two Martian weeks in bed, or, in extreme cases, in the hospital. That created other problems, because Earth Enough coverage didn't apply to Mars, where the MDC ran the hospitals for profit. But those concerns aside, people were often quite sick the moment they stepped off the craft, which is why there were plastic-lined trash cans all along the Jetway. Leonard seemed fine, as usual. The man was stronger than reinforced fiber-optic polymer. Jordan had to stop and upchuck violently on the way.

They reached the end of the Jetway and stepped onto a moving walkway, which carried them upward inside a white tube for several minutes. Every thirty seconds or so, three chimes sounded, the tube tinged red, and the words "Keep Mars Weird" appeared at intervals across the surface.

"The Martian Development Corporation welcomes you to New Austin," a soothing voice recording said. "The weirdest city on Mars. Definitely weirder than New Waco or New Bakersfield."

Jordan leaned over the moving rail and vomited once again. There were splatter-canals below in case of such an eventuality. He wasn't the only one.

"This is so incredible," Leonard said.

After what seemed like too long, they reached a platform, which was actually the hull of a giant elevator, which contained several hundred people, some of whom Jordan recognized from the flight over.

The elevator doors opened to reveal a vast entry hall, which looked like a circus tent, with its white plastic sheets overhead, billowing under the power of enormous fans, which were necessary because the hall was filled, at all times, with interstellar economy-class passengers, most of whom hadn't bathed or changed clothes the entire trip. Scattered about were MDC employees wearing navy-blue uniforms, "Keep Mars Weird" baseball caps, and little lithium-powered oxygen masks that covered their noses and mouths; they were organizing people into neat lines. A scattering of drone-bots flew overhead, filming the crowd, analyzing their movements, information that would mostly be used to make restaurant recommendations.

"Passengers from flight 134, arriving from Luna, please proceed to section 17, rows A through F," said one of the drones. "Flight 667 from Venus, please proceed to the irradiative decontamination zone for disease screening. Flight 335 from Earth—"

"That's us!" Leonard said far too chipperly.

"—please proceed to section 9, rows B through Q."

"Why not rows A through Q?" Jordan asked.

"Don't ask questions, sir," said an MDC employee. "We open up all the rows we can."

Jordan's curiosity had cost them valuable seconds. The passengers from his flight, and there were hundreds of them, stampeded toward section 9 like cattle let loose from a pen. By the time they arrived there, Jordan and Leonard were deep in the back of the pack. Every line was full. They ended up in an overflow pen, which snaked around the hall, butting up against the new groups of passengers that were continually being disgorged into the spaceport but never actually touching them. This was a very organized system. It had to be.

A drone flew overhead. "Approximate wait time from this point," it said, "four hours, twenty-five minutes."

"Ugh," Jordan said. He had no choice but to wait. On Earth, his days had been so nicely planned out, and there were never any lines, except for short ones for Friday-night ramen.

Leonard's Device sounded. He'd prepaid for Mars Minutes. "Yolo!" he said too loudly.

"Yolo, Mr. Space," Dave said, his holographic face popping out of the screen. "What are you doing?"

"Nothing mucho," said Leonard. "Just waiting in line like you."

"L-O-LLLL," Dave said. "I don't wait in line. I've been back at my house for an hour. Buzz me when you're free, and I'll take you to the coolest bar in New Austin for a drink. In twenty-four hours it will be over, but right now it is the hottest place on Mars."

"Nice," said Leonard.

"Yolo!"

"Yolo!"

Meanwhile, three more people died while waiting to go through Interplanetary Reentry. Jordan and Leonard weren't among them, though. Martian day turned to Martian night while they waited. Leonard ate the last of his Space Cakes. Jordan declined. His stomach was feeling a little off.

Finally, they reached the front of the line. Jordan went first. A functionary dressed like all the other functionaries sat in a glass booth. Overhead, the smartdrones buzzed.

"Device check," said the functionary.

Jordan produced his Device. His transit orders appeared holographically.

"Reason for coming to Mars."

"It says right there—"

"Just tell me."

"Work," said Jordan.

"What kind of work?"

"I'm a teacher."

"Hah! Good luck with that."

"Thanks."

The functionary ran a red scan over the hologram. There was a beeping noise. A polystrand gate whooshed open. Jordan stepped through.

Leonard was next. He displayed his papers.

"Reason for coming to Mars," said the functionary.

"Do I need a reason?"

"Yes. Why did you come to Mars?"

"Because I heard it was great!" Leonard said.

"Unbelievable."

"What?"

"I came here fifteen years ago for the same reason. And now I live in one room with my husband and his elderly grandmother. When I'm home. Which I never am, because I work nineteen hours a day. Let me give you some advice: turn ba—"

Overhead, a drone made a deep, loud, emergency squonking sound. It flew in over Leonard's head and smashed through the glass of the functionary's booth. A needle zipped out of its conical front cavity and moved toward the functionary's neck.

"Wait!" the functionary said. "I was just telling him—"

The needle zipped in, and the functionary crumpled to the floor. Another person appeared to replace her.

"We apologize for the politics," the replacement said. "That kind of talk has no place on Mars."

"No, it's cool," Leonard said. "Is he going to be OK?"

"Sure, kid." He ran the scanner. "Go on ahead."

The gate whooshed open for Leonard. Jordan was waiting on the other side.

"Anything wrong?" he asked.

"Nope, it's all fine," Leonard said.

But a seed had been planted in Leonard's mind that everything was not, in fact, all fine. Mars, was . . . He didn't know what Mars was. It was something else, though.

They looked about the New Austin spaceport. It was an astonishing mess of activity and color. Thousands of people were dashing about, wearing pirate hats and enormous flowers in their lapels. There were restaurants of every cuisine imaginable, and all of them had lines of at least a hundred people to get in. Enormous holograms zipped around at an equally frenzied pace overhead, entertaining and advertising simultaneously. The MDC logo was everywhere. On a raised stage, a guitar band was playing a song.

Keep Mars Weird.

Keep Mars Weird.

Grow out your beard,
And Keep Mars Weird.

As the song said, many of the people, male, female, or indeterminate, had spectacular beards, which spread across their chests like wheat. Some of them had their beards done up in ornate braids. Leonard saw one man run by with what appeared to be two live miniature bears living in his beard folds. Leonard and Jordan, standing there relatively clean shaven in their dirty Earth unitards, stared at the passing scene gape mouthed. Everyone looked so different, and yet they looked the same.

A voice boomed. "TREND ALERT!"

Everyone in the terminal stopped to look at their Devices.

"Ladies and gentlemen," it said. "The flowers have wilted. Take off those boutonnieres if you want to remain fashionable."

Instantly, thousands of people dashed their lovingly grown flowers to the floor.

"Also, it's time to shear the sheep. Martian summer is coming. And that means no more beards."

The band played:

Keep Mars Weird.
Keep Mars Weird.
Shave off your beard,
And Keep Mars Weird.

There was a barbershop on an upper level. The people in the terminal charged upstairs. The barber's face filled with terror. A thousand panicked trendsters looked his way.

"Shave yourselves!" the barber cried as he slammed down the shutters.

"Beard stampede!" Leonard shouted. The people were charging in all directions, looking for solar razors, any sharp blade, really. Jordan and Leonard ran in the opposite direction, toward the exit.

"I hate spaceports," Jordan said, and they walked into the Martian night.

12

They waited an hour and a half for a hover-cab. The air felt thick. Jordan found himself getting dizzy. He felt light, as though his bones were about to float out of his body.

"Where's the solar-powered über-train?" he asked, to no one in particular. Leonard didn't seem concerned. He'd been absorbed in a holographic Wacky Farm scenario on his Device.

The person in front of Jordan said, "The MDC killed the spaceport train. They said people preferred personal freedom to collectivism."

"Do they?"

"Who knows?" said the guy. "I'm a person, and I think a train would be nice."

Finally Jordan and Leonard got into a hover-cab. It was dank and sticky inside.

"Where to?" the cabbie said.

Jordan looked at his Device, which had all the information he needed about the teachers' dorm.

"Seventy-One New Austin Plaza."

"Shit, that's downtown. Driving down there is a fucking nightmare. Flat rate of six thousand seven hundred and seventy-seven credits."

"Did you say six *thousand* and seven hundred and seventy-seven?"

"Yeah, we pass through like ten tolls. It adds up."

That was as much as Jordan spent in a month on Earth, on everything combined. But it's not like he had any choice.

"Fine," he sighed.

"What about you, buddy?" the cabbie said to Leonard. "Where are you headed?"

"Oh, wherever he's going is fine," Leonard said.

"Don't you have a place to stay?" Jordan asked.

"I figured I'd just crash with you until I figure things out."

"But I'm staying in a *dormitory.* I—never mind, just drive."

The cabbie started the meter.

They drove for miles and miles. The traffic was more congested than anything Jordan had ever witnessed. There'd be a four- or five-minute stretch of open air and then a huge logjam. The cabbie swooped and snaked where he could, but the skyways were an inexplicable mess of lanes and on-ramps, designed by idiots, thrown up for no other reason than to access housing complexes that shot up out of nowhere.

Vast straight stretches of hover-way gave them a chance to see their new surroundings. Everywhere you looked, New Austin, even at midnight, was nothing but a sea of personal vehicles, all of them creeping along, frustrated, headed toward nowhere in particular. No one had told Jordan that Mars was so *ugly.*

At one point, when the traffic ensnared the hover-cab, little children, their faces smeared with dirt, appeared out of nowhere and approached the car on the hover-way, bearing packets of chewing gum and bags of fruit. The cabbie pressed a button, and a violent blast of air came out of the cab's side, blowing the kids onto the median.

"Give in to one," he said, "and you gotta give in to them all."

The roadsides were dotted with houses—Jordan guessed you could call them houses—made of paper and reclaimed metal, with burnt-out hover-car hulks in front of them. Even at this late hour, gaunt, wasted-looking men and women sat there in the red dirt and soot, picking their teeth, gazing at the passing traffic with dead, unblinking eyes. They didn't have Enough.

Finally, on the horizon, downtown New Austin appeared, an endlessly stretching line of shining skyscrapers framed by swooping klieg lights. In every direction, Jordan saw cranes, swirling, building, lifting, creating the greatest city the universe had ever known. The sky exploded with light.

"Fireworks!" Leonard said.

It was some sort of display, all right. The rockets boomed and crackled and whistled, and when it was all over, the words "Keep Mars Weird" exploded in the night sky.

After an hour-long wait at an on-ramp, they made the approach into downtown. Neon-lit bars and restaurants, all of which had long lines of flowerless, freshly shaven men and women out front, lined the canyon-like streets. It was the middle of the night, and everything was packed. Music blared out of every doorway. Waves of tourists, unencumbered by traffic because it was all across the skyway, stumbled around, chugging on foot-tall drinks and eating enormous sausages of questionable origin.

The cabbie turned into a square that was slightly quieter than the melee they'd just passed through. He parked in front of a low-lying tan structure, almost unimaginably ugly, that looked like a discarded shoe among all the glitz.

"New Austin Plaza," he said.

"This is it?" Jordan said. "I figured a teacher's dorm—"

"Hah!" said the cabbie. "You're a *teacher*? You're lucky they let you go downtown at all."

They paid their fare. Jordan felt physical pain, it was so expensive. The cabbie didn't help them haul their bags.

A tired-looking security guard was sitting at the desk of the teacher's dorm.

"Can I help you?" he moaned.

"Jordan Kincaid. I'm here for my housing."

"Who's this?" he said, pointing at Leonard.

"I'm just gonna crash here for a while, too," Leonard said. "If that's cool."

"Suit yourself. It's ten thousand a month for a bunk."

"I'll check it out," Leonard said, while thinking, *I'm not paying ten thousand a month for anything.*

They took a creaky elevator up a couple of floors. The elevator smelled like sweat and piss. The hall it disgorged them into was undecorated, lit by flickering fluorescent bulbs, and it smelled just like the elevator.

Jordan and Leonard came to a steel door that read "Bunkroom 12."

"Shit," Jordan said. "I don't have a key."

"I don't think you need one," Leonard said as he pushed open the door.

The dank, windowless room was barely larger than Jordan's room back on Earth, but there were a dozen bunks in it, lined floor to ceiling. In a far corner, separated from the room only by a torn, three-paneled screen, was a toilet and sink illuminated by the room's only, flickering light. Jordan could see someone squatting on the pot.

People of indeterminate gender occupied ten of the bunks, though Jordan guessed that, by the volume of their snoring, they were all at least partially male. He heard a loud farting noise from behind the screen, and then some scritching around, and then a big sigh, and a trickle of water. A shambling wreck of a man, dressed nearly in rags, emerged and made his way to them.

"You Kincaid?" he said, extending a hand.

Jordan shook his hand, reluctantly. He didn't know where that hand had been, or if it had been washed in a while.

"We've been waiting for you for a few days," the man said. "Trouble getting in?"

"Yeah," Jordan said.

"Typical. Well, we saved you a bunk." He waved his hand toward a bottom bed, near the door, topped with a thin, soiled mattress. "No sheets, though. We were supposed to get some from the MDC, but they keep delaying delivery."

Jordan grimaced. "That's OK," he said. "Where do I put my stuff?"

The guy looked at Jordan quizzically. "On the bunk," he said.

"There's nowhere to plug in my Device."

"Hah! You can do that at work. Most of the schools have outlets."

Leonard was furiously waving at his Device. Dave Waters's face had appeared.

"Yolo!" he said.

"Take it into the hall," said the dorm monitor.

Leonard did. "Dude," he said. "You've got to get me out of here. This teachers' dorm is *trash*."

"L-O-LLLLLL!" Dave said, too loudly, obviously flying high on Mars Dust. "I could have told you that. Teachers live like shit. You can crash with me until you get a gig."

"Thanks, man."

"What are you guys doing right now?" Dave asked.

"Hang on," Leonard said.

He gestured into the dorm room, where Jordan was trying to figure out how he would ever get comfortable again. Jordan came out.

"Yolo!" said Dave, looking at Jordan expectantly.

"Yolo," Jordan sighed.

"You look like crap."

"Thanks."

"Dudes, meet me at the Hungry Hat in like fifteen minutes."

"I'm pretty tired . . ." Jordan said.

"Don't be deadweight!" said Dave. "You're on Mars, let's party! There's a band going on at three thirty a.m. that you will *love*."

Jordan's Device lit up with the address of the Hungry Hat. It was, mercifully, quite nearby.

They walked there. Staggering humans packed the streets of New Austin, wearing the latest fashions. Food stalls sold every manner of delicacy. One of them advertised Neo-Malaysian food, and there hadn't been an actual Malaysia in nearly three hundred years. Jordan bookmarked "Infinite Crust Pizza" as something to definitely try later.

They got to the Hungry Hat within fifteen minutes. It took the entire ground floor of a soaring skyscraper. At least a thousand people waited outside.

"Dude, we're never getting into this," said Leonard.

From the front, Dave Waters waved to them. He wore a ski cap knitted in the shape of a chicken head and a neon-purple shirt with the nipples cut out, and what looked like surprisingly ordinary denim pants until Jordan got up close and could see that they were, in fact, spray-painted on, over what appeared to be the skimpiest possible briefs. What's more, now that he looked, he saw that dozens of other people were also showing off their denim-spangled crotches. The temperature in New Austin was always a steady seventy-four degrees Fahrenheit (more in high-emissions zones), so hanging loose was a frequent sartorial option.

"Yolo, my brothers!" he said. "Come on in!"

"Yolo!" Leonard said.

"But the line . . . ," Jordan said.

"Friends of mine never have to wait at the Hungry Hat!" Dave said. "I own this bar! Well, really, I manage it for investor friends of my dad. I'm in charge."

Jordan and Leonard shuffled past the line as the crowd grumbled. There were even a couple of muffled boos. But they got in.

Curtains parted, revealing a velvet-tinged lounge of substantial proportions. Music was thumping from an adjacent room.

"There are like three bands before the Walking Whispers," Dave said. "You guys'll love them. They have a drummer *from Luna*."

"Yolo!" Leonard said. "Lunar music is really authentic."

He might have added "gritty" and "real." Luna produced some tough drummers. And some pretty decent front men, too.

The clientele, as at rock clubs throughout the eons, appeared to be mostly men, with the occasional bored-looking woman standing around checking her Device. Long-legged waitresses strolled about with trays of drinks and joints and little velour bags of Mars Dust—all the pleasures that inherited credits could buy. Dave walked them through the bar. He removed a slender rope from behind a booth and snuggled them in next to him.

"This is my domain," Dave said. "Yolo!"

A loud crack sounded from the back of the bar. Dave's head exploded. A chunk of his brains landed in Jordan's lap. Jordan rasped. Leonard leapt to his feet.

And that's when the bar blew up.

13

Richard Waters, the president, CEO, cofounder, and sole presiding board member of the Mars Development Corporation, a for-profit company where he received all the profits (which was totally legal because of a law that he'd written for the Martian Senate, which had been elected thanks to his campaign donations), had removed his toupee for bed and was getting ready to remove his spot-free epidermis covering as well. He did that. Within a minute, he'd also removed his false blue irises, false black eyebrows, and an upper row of teeth, which some damn anarchist had knocked out years ago during the First Olympus Mons campaign.

Waters unzipped his man-corset and let out a massive fart as his belly escaped. Almost instantaneously, he was transformed from a tan, fit captain of industry into a sad old man. With the help of his team of topflight doctors, imported from Earth because he was no idiot, Waters had developed a new regimen.

For thirty-six hours a week, consecutively, he lay in a hyperbaric ultraviolet float, soothed by chimes and waves and the morning sounds of mountain meadows. Everything had been engineered for double the sleep effects. This meant that he could then stay awake for the rest of the week, leaving him plenty of time to buy property and take over companies and build luxury hotels and go about shaping Mars in the image of Dick Waters, the greatest businessperson that the galaxy had ever known. His health-and-mental-preservation plan, like his sleeping chamber, had no holes. Even so, as he continued to fortify his brain with every essential and pricey acid solution on the market, slippage had begun.

Just as Waters prepared to summon his medical team for his bedtime rituals (a digital enema tube was involved), his Device shuddered. This was his private Device, not the public one he showily and constantly used to browbeat moronic politicians and timorous small-property owners. Only four people had this connection—his two children, his accountant, and his chief of security—so when it summoned, he usually had to answer.

"*What?*" he shouted grumpily. He'd just finished the journey from Earth. Even at the very height of human luxury, that trip aged a man. He often had to make it twice a year, with very little turnaround time on Earth. He needed his sleep regimen more than ever.

It was his daughter, Crystal.

"Daddy," she gasped. The sight of Waters's withered true form could have that effect.

Waters drew a blanket around himself and popped in his teeth. "This had better be important."

"It is. There's been a bombing in the rave district. Seven dead, more than that injured."

"Another one?" said Waters. "Who was it this time? The People's Revolutionary Front? The Populist People's Brigade? The Pedicycleanarchist Workers Army?"

"No one group has taken credit. But they're all made up of the same people anyway."

"Well, goddamn it, have the cops raid a hideout and put a couple of them to death."

Crystal looked uncomfortable.

"What?" Waters said impatiently. He could feel his colon begin to gurgle. That enema had to come soon.

"The bombing happened at the Hungry Hat."

"What the hell is that?"

"It's a club."

"What the hell kind of name is that for a club? In my day, clubs had classy names, like the Cabana Room or Edie's Hideaway."

"It's the one that Dave manages," she said.

"Goddamn it," Waters said.

David was such an *idiot.* He always skimped on security. Waters had raised him to hoard money, but all David could do was spend. And blow it up his nose. Enough of this club nonsense. Waters was revoking nightlife privileges. His boy could start coming to work with him, like a real man.

"Tell David I'll speak to him in the morning," Waters said. "And update me in thirty-six hours if you find anything."

But Crystal's visage did not shut down.

"May I *help* you?" Waters snarled.

"Well . . ."

"Just *say* it!"

"They haven't found Dave yet, and I'm getting worried."

I really just want to sleep, Waters thought. But this was his only son. If he was actually dead, it wouldn't look good if the most powerful man on Mars, possibly in human history, slept through his own son's wake. He sighed and reached for his fake skin.

"I'll be there in ten minutes," he said.

14

Waters had his driver leave him a block and a half from the scene. He knew it was bad optics on a world where most people couldn't even afford their own bicycles, to pull up at the scene of a terrorist bombing in a bespoke sports limo.

The streets were choked with young people wearing ridiculous nonsense, like fake raccoon tails made out of actual raccoon fur. They didn't seem to be having much fun. They chattered nervously, stared at their Devices, waited in line.

Why does anyone actually want to live here? Waters thought, but he knew the answer. He'd spent millions upon millions of credits to brainwash them into thinking Mars was cool. They didn't know another way, and Waters wanted to make sure it stayed like that forever.

The streets around the Hungry Hat had been completely barricaded for a half block in every direction. Crystal was waiting for Waters at the eastern barricade. She'd landed her little white convertible hover-car right at the scene. She'd driven it over the barricades herself. Crystal didn't worry about getting hassled by the anarchists. Even *they* wanted to party with her.

"There's a lot of smoke," she warned.

"You think I haven't inhaled bomb debris before?" Waters said. "I came to Mars the year you were born. This place hasn't known a month without a major bombing since."

"Right, but . . ."

Waters moved through the barricade. No one dared stop him. They knew who he was. Crystal followed behind nervously.

The front of the club had been blown completely inward. Smoke still billowed from inside. The sidewalk was riddled with polymer shards and leather. Emergency men were still charging into the building and emerging with young people, moaning and weeping in pain, some of them on stretchers, others just clutching body parts and looking miserable.

This was way worse than usual. The resistance had upgraded.

"Lucky only seven people died in this," Waters said.

"Actually, they're saying seventy. Maybe more."

"Don't say seven when you mean seventy. That's a sixty-three-person difference!"

"I know, Daddy," she said. "That was the best information at the time."

The MDC was going to have to pay death benefits to the families of all the victims, substantial ones. That was the only equality law still in play on Mars, the last piece of the obsolete Terran safety net. The Earth government would not bend on that.

"Have they found Dave yet?" he asked. "Dead or alive?"

"Some people said they saw him earlier and said if we see him alive have him call them because they're having a VIP party later."

"By Gaia's filthy cunt!" he said. "Find him!"

"You shouldn't take the goddess's vagina in vain," Crystal said.

"Sorry," he said.

"I'm upset, too," she said. "Who'd have thought someone would want to bomb the Hungry Hat? Poor David."

A figure, filthy and staggering and holding a half-crisped pirate's hat, emerged from the rubble. It bent double, then collapsed.

"Jordan!" Crystal shouted. She ran over to him.

Jordan Kincaid lay on the ground. Crystal knelt.

"Hello, Crystal," he moaned.

"Oh, Jordan, Jordan, you poor dear," she said. "Does it hurt very much?"

"I think I'm OK," he said. "Now that you're here."

"Aren't you sweet," she said. "We're going to take good care of you."

Crystal looked him over. There were some minor cuts and burns. His uniform had been torn to shreds. And his legs were covered with viscera.

"What is that?" she said.

"That is your brother's brains," he said.

Crystal screamed.

♦ ♦ ♦

Crystal recovered quickly. She arranged to get Jordan patched in the VIP health module, to avoid waiting. By the time Crystal came to see him, he was already pretty well healed. There'd even been time for a hairdresser. He looked nice and clean and handsome.

"Well, hello there!" he said.

"You seem pretty chipper for someone who just almost got killed."

"They gave me two hundred milligrams of THC."

"Yeah, me, too."

Crystal sat next to Jordan on the bed and sighed. "Oh, Jordan," she said. "What are we going to *do*?"

"I don't know," he said. "I have no idea what's going on. I've only been on Mars for twelve hours, and I haven't even slept yet."

"You poor dear," she said. "Coming over here in the middle of all this. Where are you staying?"

"I'm nearby," he said. "At the teachers' dorm."

"*The teachers' dorm?*" she said. "You can't stay there, Jordan. There was a cholera outbreak at the teachers' dorm just last month. Half the schools on the planet still haven't reopened."

"Oh," he said. "But that's where I'm staying."

"You are most certainly not," she said. "You are going to stay with me. Until you can get your own place, which, if you're working as a teacher, is never."

"But, I couldn't take up space in your bed . . ."

"Don't be silly," she said. "I have a guest suite downstairs, and you'll be able to come and go as you please, with a separate entrance and exit. *I'll* let you know when and if you can come visit. Right now, I'm in mourning." She gave him her hand. "Come, dear."

A couple of hours had passed and the chaos had lessened a bit. The final death toll had actually turned out to be only forty-three, which didn't even put it in the top ten of all time. Dick Waters's face hovered over the block. "We condemn this cowardly act, and we will bring those responsible for it to justice," he was saying.

The recorded message was five years old, and they played it every time. The actual Dick Waters was already in his hibernation chamber. No one noticed. Most of them were flying on Mars Dust for weeks at a time. The crowd just ignored it and moved on to the next party.

"This is the most dreadful day," Crystal said. "At least Daddy's not turning David into a martyr."

He wouldn't make a very sympathetic one, she thought. Her brother had been a harmless goof, but he was also a walking poster for inequality. The people of Mars were already fully aware of what they didn't have. They didn't need any more reminders. But no matter what, this was going to draw focus to the revolutionary cause. Some people bought into this crap. She made a note to herself to lower Mars Dust prices 15 percent, at least temporarily.

Jordan got into her hover-car. He settled into the nice leather, which felt so comfortable that it made him feel uncomfortable. Now he'd seen how Martians lived. He didn't know if he wanted to be party to this reality. Then again, he really wanted to be with Crystal.

"Nice wheels," he said.

"They're leased," she said. "Like everything else. Let's go home."

"What about my things?"

"Have the teachers' dorm burn them. They're just Earth junk."

She lifted up toward the clouds, to a first-class altitude that few vehicles were allowed to broach.

"We're going to get you lots of new things," she said.

She tossed him a bag of Mars Dust. Jordan inhaled it eagerly, leaned back, and sighed. Sure, he'd had his friend's brains dumped into his lap just a few hours earlier, but things were actually turning out pretty well on old Mars. Then he realized he'd forgotten something very important.

"Wait," he said. "What about Leonard?"

15

Leonard Tolliver woke up in a cave, or a basement, or a cave-like basement. He heard water dripping. His skin felt brittle, his mouth dusty. Leonard tried to sit up. His skull played the drums.

Something was pressing Leonard down. He opened his eyes. Even though his vision was blurred, he could see that he was on some sort of cot, under a big pile of blankets. He was feeling a lot of things. Cold wasn't one of them.

"Can you hear me?" a voice said.

Leonard looked over to his left. A gaunt man in a drab olive jumpsuit sat in a chair beside him, a plastic tub in his lap. The man dipped a rag into the tub, pulled it out, and wrung it.

"Y-yes," Leonard said.

"How are you feeling?" the man said.

"Tired," Leonard said honestly.

The man daubed Leonard's head with the rag. The moisture felt good. It relieved the hammer in Leonard's brain, just a little.

"That's understandable," the man said. "You've had quite an ordeal."

Suddenly, Leonard remembered everything: the endless journey to Mars, going into the bar, meeting Dave, Dave's head splattering, and then the explosion—

He sat upright. A sharp pain shot through his midsection. His head felt both jangly and leaden.

"Where am I?"

The man gently pushed Leonard back down. "Take it easy, you're safe. And it looks like you're going to recover fully."

"But where *am* I?" Leonard insisted. "Am I still on Mars?"

"Of course you are," said the man. "Where else would you be?"

Leonard suddenly realized that this strange cot in this dank room was the first bed he'd slept in on Mars. He hoped it wouldn't be his last. And he knew he wasn't hallucinating; no drug could ever leave him *this* disoriented.

"Where's Jordan?"

"Jordan who?" said the man, who Leonard guessed was some sort of nurse.

"Jordan Kincaid, my *room—*" But they didn't live together anymore. "My friend."

"I don't know any Jordan Kincaid. Is he in your platoon?"

"My platoon?"

"Of your sector."

"My sector?"

"You know, your sector of your company? Which building are you from?"

"What company? What building? What are you talking about? Who are you? Where the fuck *am* I?"

Leonard's nurse looked at him sympathetically. "You really don't know, do you?"

"No!" Leonard shouted.

"You poor thing, you lost all your memory in the blast."

"I didn't lose my memory! I remember everything! I just have no idea what you're talking about! What *is* this place?"

"You're in a field hospital of the Martian Resistance Army."

"The *what*?"

"The MRA. The rebel force that is trying to protect Mars from being overrun by the scumbag developers."

"I have never heard of the MRA," Leonard said.

The nurse looked at him for a hard second and then stood up. "Don't go anywhere," he said, chuckling. He stood up and walked away.

The room was silent for a while. Then Leonard heard a low moan, from just a few feet away. He looked over. A young woman was on a cot identical to his. She swatted at the air. There was a bandaged stump where her left leg should have been. Her moans grew louder and more desperate. She thrashed and flailed, and then she collapsed in a heap.

This was not at all what Leonard had expected. Mars was supposed to be awesome.

Leonard heard footsteps. His nurse trailed behind a powerful-looking woman in a vicious dust-red sleeveless tank top. Sonia Smartphone, the head of the Martian Resistance Army, pounded the floor with her massive boots. Sonia wore her cargo pants heavy, wore her hair short, and wore her face in an incessant scowl, somewhere between extreme concern and uncontrolled anger.

In a few broad, confident strides, Sonia marched up to Leonard. She grabbed his shirt collar and lifted him out of bed.

"Hey!" Leonard said. "Quit it!"

Leonard dangled from her hand like a puppet. He'd lost a lot of weight. His headache was suddenly the least of his troubles.

"You have ten seconds to explain yourself before I kill you," she said.

Leonard could see that she was serious, so he blurted, "My name is Leonard Tolliver, I'm from Earth, I just got to Mars, and I was at a bar that got bombed, that's all."

She lowered him. His legs felt unsteady, and he staggered into her. Sonia grasped him before he fell. Her chest was sweaty, but her arms were strong. She pushed him down into his bed.

"You're from Earth," she said.

"Yep."

"And you just got to Mars."

"Depends on how long I've been here."

"One of our operatives pulled you out of the rubble. He thought you were one of ours. You've been unconscious here for eight days."

"Then I've been on Mars for eight days," Leonard said.

"That's it?"

"That's it."

"Where are you staying? Why are you here?"

"I'm here to party!" Leonard said. "Or at least I was. I heard Mars was awesome."

"That's just what the MDC wants you to hear," she said. "They need rich Earth dupes like you who'll pay the rents on all those shoddy condos they're building."

"I'm not rich," Leonard said. "I just have Enough, like everyone."

"On Mars, that makes you rich," Sonia said. "No one here has anything. The MDC has it all."

"You know, I was noticing that on the flight over. When we visited our friend Dave in Executive—"

"Dave?" she said.

"David Waters. You know, the guy whose head you blew off."

Sonia lifted Leonard by his collar again. "You know David Waters?" she said.

"Erk," said Leonard.

"Son of Richard Waters, the head of the Mars Development Corporation, the whole reason this entire planet is a hellish suck-hole?"

"Blerg."

She put Leonard down. A sonic pellet gun came out of her holster. "Then I *am* going to have to kill you," she said.

"Wait wait wait wait wait wait wait wait wait!" Leonard said. "You can't kill me. I'm innocent!"

"No one is innocent on Mars."

"I am. I really am. I don't have any idea what you're talking about. At all. If you're going to kill me, at least you can tell me why."

Sonia sat down in her chair and sighed. "It's a long story," she said.

"Does it look like I have much else to do?" Leonard said.

"Fine," she said. "But I'm still going to kill you when it's done."

"At least I'll get to spend my last moments listening to you talk."

Sonia pulled the gun and nudged it up under Leonard's chin. "Don't fuck with me, Earthboy," she said.

"I have never fucked with anyone. Ever."

"OK," she said. "Here's the deal. Thirty years ago, Mars was a pretty nice place to live. I mean, it was a dirty shit-hole backwater, but it was *cheap*. There was *art*. People were alive. You could do what you want, you know? But it was starting to get overcrowded. Families were stacking up in the original developments, four or five families to an apartment. There was disease. People were getting murdered, getting raped. It was real shit. Bad shit, but it was *inspiring*, you know?"

"I'm sure," Leonard said.

"Shut up," said Sonia. "The music was good. Raw. It had an edge, not like the shit people listen to now, all that 'make some fucking noise' club crap. Still, something had to change, because of the Earth rats and the gangs and the garbage strike and all."

Leonard had no idea what she was talking about, but he was trying to forestall his murder and was also still trying to figure out where he was and what was happening to him. And also, she was hot. He could listen to her talk all day long.

"Then the MDC showed up, and it all went to hell," she said. "They wanted to build these towers."

"What towers?"

"The towers you're in right now. Seven of them, twenty stories high. They had to get a dome variance and had to import half the materials from Earth, and the towers took years to build, but they were determined. This was the best way to ensure that everyone had Enough. And, you know, the towers weren't fancy, and they got dirty very fast, and the Mars Dust syndicate took over three of them within the first year. But they got a lot of families in them. The towers worked pretty well. The MDC did their job OK.

"But then Dick Waters took control of them. He started manipulating the Martian Congress. At first it was just a zoning variance here and there, teardowns of old fuel-cell stations. Sure, they were art co-ops, but not very successful ones. Gradually, the MDC started buying up all the properties, putting up fancy buildings with fancy security, jacking up rents. Wages didn't keep up, and gradually Mars began to change. All these Earthpeople started coming in and 'investing.' They'd buy property for what was a fortune to Martians, tear down the structures, and put up new buildings. The people in them wore these ridiculous clothes and started going to these ridiculous clubs and driving these ridiculous pink scooters. Mars started getting fancy. There were people at the MDC who thought this was a bad idea. They wanted it to be like Earth, where everyone had Enough. But Waters was greedy. He forced everyone else out. All the graffiti was gone, all the old businesses were gone, all that crazy ingenuity that poverty breeds in a population was gone, and in its place was nothing but shiny buildings and fancy restaurants and traffic."

"Sounds awful," Leonard said.

"It sounds like it happened overnight," she said. "But it didn't."

The nurse dude interjected. "By the time I got to Mars—"

"You're not from here?" Leonard said, surprised.

"No, I came from Earth six years ago. I was bored there in New Beijing, where I was from. All those blue skies and animal parks and crystal-clean coastal reserves and everyone singing the 'I Love the Earth' song every day. Earth was lame. I wanted to get out into the galaxy, have some adventure, you know?"

"Oh, I know," Leonard said.

"And so I was reading about Mars," he said, "seeing all these videos about this funky alternative culture, all this amazing art. It seemed like a place where people could be creative, could be themselves, you know? Keep Mars Weird and all that. And then I get here and I find out that Keep Mars Weird is nothing but a stupid *real estate slogan.* It was bad. I got an apartment in South New Austin with four other people. The deposit cost me half my Earth savings, so I had to take a job carting pansexual clubgoers around in a pedi-scooter. It really built up my calf muscles. But the company didn't pay. I could only work for tips, and half the time the people were too drunk to tip me. So I ran out of money. Then I had to move to North New Austin, and I had to take the public hover-bus to work. But the buses only came twice a day and they were usually full, so I missed work three days in a row and I got fired. I figured I'd come to Mars and find something fresh and artsy, but I was so tired and broke all the time that I didn't have a creative thought in my head.

"Finally one day I got fed up. I heard there was going to be a development protest against the MDC, so I went to see what was going on. People were singing and banging drums and chanting slogans and painting signs, and I thought, well, this is the community I've been looking for, right? But then the MDC sent their goons in to bust up the protest, and I saw friends, people I'd worked with, *comrades*, getting dragged off to jail or worse."

"Worse?" Leonard said.

"Yeah, man," said Sonia. "They cut off a protestor's head. Everyone saw it on their Devices. They said, 'This is what happens when you don't Keep Mars Weird.'"

"That is fucked *up*," said Leonard. "Did they really do that?"

"I recorded it," Sonia said. "We all did. No one in New Austin remembers it because they're so messed up on Mars Dust that they don't remember *anything*. But we stay clean. It's required if you want to join the Resistance Army."

"Wait," he said. "There are no drugs here. At *all*?"

"I mean, we have cannabis," said Sonia. "For Gaia's sake, we're not savages. But none of that synthetic crap."

"That's good."

"The MDC won't stop. They want to own *everything*. These towers are the last major undeveloped property in New Austin. No one lives here anymore, not legally. The MDC had them condemned eighteen months ago. But they're still communal property. It's all tied up in the Earth courts, and they're never going to untangle the mess. So we live here. We play music, make art, have sex."

"Sounds good!" Leonard said.

"And stockpile weapons. The Resistance Army is going to rise."

Leonard sighed. "Man, Mars is fucked up."

"We will take it back," Sonia said. "For the people. And now that you know the truth . . ."

She raised her pellet gun and cocked the trigger.

"Hang on!" Leonard said. "I can help!"

"How?"

"I don't know," he said. "I like revolutions, maybe?"

"Do you have any weapons skills?"

"No."

"Do you have any fighting-arts skills?"

"No."

"Can you play inspirational instruments?"

"Gaia no!"

"Do you have any medical training or knowledge about below-ground hydroponic agriculture?"

"No."

"What skills *do* you have?"

"I have seen every episode of *The Incredible Holographic Mangapus.* Including the lost ones from the twenty-second century."

She sighed. "I have to kill you. You've seen the inside of our headquarters. If we let you back into New Austin, who knows who you might tell."

"I will tell *no one*! I swear!"

"They have psychotropic confession drugs."

"Cool!"

She raised the gun again. "We will not jeopardize Ruben Kincaid's vision of a Mars where everyone has Enough. The people's planet will rise!"

"Wait, did you say Ruben Kincaid? Like Jordan Kincaid's father?"

"I don't know any Jordan Kincaid."

"I do. He's my roommate. He *was* my roommate. We came to Mars together."

Sonia put the gun to his head. "You're *lying*," she said.

"No, no, I'm not. Give me my Device and I'll prove it to you."

Sonia nodded to the nurse, who walked over to a cabinet, reached inside, and got Leonard's Device, which, according to Earth manufacturing standards, had been built to survive a nuclear blast, much less a standard terrorist bomb.

Leonard turned on his Device. The Mangapus appeared, singing his Mangapus song. Sonia fired a pellet into the wall above Leonard's head.

"OK!" Leonard said. "OK."

He called up Jordan's avatar. Jordan rotated in a circle. Underneath sat his name, "Jordan Kincaid."

"See?" he said. "I know him."

"Message him," Sonia said. "Prove it."

"Now?" Leonard said. "But he can trace you."

"We've disabled tracers here. He'll have no idea where you are."

"OK," Leonard said.

"Hey," he messaged to Jordan.

Fifteen seconds passed. Sonia kept the gun at Leonard's head. And then the holographic words appeared: "WHERE ARE YOU?"

"I'm OK," Leonard messaged back. "Don't worry. Hey, BTW, are you Jordan Kincaid, son of Ruben Kincaid?"

"You know I am," Jordan said.

"Cool, CYU later."

"WAIT," Jordan texted back.

Sonia shut off Leonard's Device.

"See?" Leonard said.

She lowered the gun. "We may have some use for you after all," she said.

16

Jordan Kincaid sat at his desk in his wobbly chair, his eyes rimmed red with exhaustion, a three-day growth of beard spreading across his face like a fungus. He looked out into the dank room, lit by flickering fluorescence, where fifty-two children of various ages sat on ancient benches, looking glassily at their Devices. Jordan was only allowed to teach every day from a preprepared script. The children followed along dully, little rivulets of drool forming on their chins. If one of them attempted to fidget or display an independent thought, Jordan was deputized to give them a Calming Injection.

"Repeat after me," he said, reading from his script and only from his script. "In 2553, the MDC brought freedom and economic opportunity to all of Mars."

"In 2553, MDC brought tunity to Mars," the children mumbled.

"Everyone was now allowed to work and own property based on their ability."

"Work propability," the children said.

This was something they had to recite every Thursday, so they were a little less than enthusiastic. In fact, you could say they were that way about everything. The MDC only cared that the children could read at a level sufficient for them to shop on their Devices and to follow written instructions. They all worked part-time at garment factories and abattoirs after school so they could have money to buy the things they made. By going to school, they got access to good entry-level jobs, like slinging ice cream or repairing broken holo-cubes. That gave them valuable experience while they pursued their mostly crushed dreams during their very limited spare time. The MDC taught that inequality was the surest sign of economic progress.

"Through hard work," Jordan said, "everyone can afford a nice place to live and we can Keep Mars Weird."

"Work hard to live," said the children. "Keep Mars Weird."

Most of these kids lived with three or four families in two-room apartments on the very edge of the domed area, where the foul, brutal Martian winds rattled the windows every night and the dust crept through the floorboards like a sinister virus. For this privilege, they paid rent equivalent to an entire Earth year's salary. They did not have Enough.

The horn rang, low and slow.

"That's all," Jordan said to the kids. "Tomorrow we'll have math and we'll watch a video about animals."

"Math" was a lesson about how to operate mobile cash-swipe chips. The animal video was actually an employee ad for a company that sold synthetic animal companions to rich retirees. But Jordan had no choice because that was the script.

The children trudged wordlessly to the exit, back to their sweatshops or their hovels or the pharmaceutical personality-adjustment clinics that operated free daycare in exchange for unpaid juvenile drug trials. Jordan felt equally numb. He closed his script tablet and put it in the unlocked desk. No one was going to steal it.

From the desk drawer, he pulled a little bag of Mars Dust. It had been six hours since his last dose, and it had worn off long ago. He felt raw and dull. His teeth ached.

Jordan stuck his nose in the little velvet bag and huffed. Quickly, he felt the familiar head tingle and warmth in his chest. By the time he stood up and left the room, he was soaringly ecstatic, feeling like he could fly to Jupiter by himself. His brain fired, not with ideas, necessarily, but with happiness. Since happiness seemed to be in short supply on Mars, he was happy to feel it. He floated through the hallways, through a sea of students and miserable teachers, out the front door, and into the private shuttle transfer that awaited him, driven by the best-trained MDC security personnel.

"Good afternoon, Mr. Kincaid," said the driver. "How was your day?"

"Great!" Jordan said. Even though it hadn't been, it was better now and would get even better soon.

Usually by the time teachers had been on Mars for a few months, they were usually wearing the equivalent of sackcloth, broke enough to resort to begging for food money after work or giving weekend "sessions" at neighborhood-sanctioned pangendered oral sex parlors. But Jordan lived at Crystal Waters's rent free. Crystal dressed him like a doll, in the most fashionable pants and hats. He also got his own en suite bedroom, access to a full kitchen, and all the Mars Dust and cannabis he could consume. He definitely had Enough; he had more than he'd bargained for.

It was an easy cruise home. It would have taken seventy-five minutes to two hours in ordinary traffic, but MDC vehicles got to hover above, in private toll lanes. Cars that tried to enter without permission would be vaporized. Because of that, Jordan got to the penthouse in ten minutes.

The door opened, and Jordan stepped into the foyer. Crystal was lying on a synthetic-fur chaise, her soft-touch robe open from the breast to the navel. She worked irregular hours, doing unknowable things. Sometimes she'd be gone all day. Other times, she'd stay in her private chambers for forty-eight hours straight, receiving visitors who weren't Jordan, who would talk to her in low, serious voices. And then sometimes, she made herself very available.

"Look at you," she said. "Cute as a poodle and hung like a moose."

The Mars Dust always gave Jordan a massive erection. So did Crystal. The two together were an unstoppable combination. His engorged tensor rod threatened to rip apart the synthetic crotch of his stylish Fabri-pants.

"How was work, big boy?" she said.

"Terrible," Jordan said.

With her, he could be honest.

Crystal opened her arms wide. Her gown fell open, revealing her round breasts, full hips, and pulsating mound, which she'd greased up with Glisten-O, a special Mars Dust–based lubricant that increased sexual pleasure. Jordan leapt upon her like a well-trained pet.

Sex on Mars Dust always got frantic. The drug responded to friction. They rolled around and rubbed, generating heat. Crystal had had them both injected with a questionable supplement that increased the intensity and duration of orgasms tenfold. It was hard to know exactly when the coming began and when it ended. Tonight, as always, pretty much from the moment Jordan touched her, ecstasy convulsed him, and it continued like that for what seemed like hours but was actually twenty-three and a half minutes, when he exploded like a hellish geyser all over Crystal's belly.

They lay together on the floor, heaving. Crystal reached over, grabbed Jordan's pants, and wiped herself with them. It didn't matter. He had ten identical pairs in his closet.

Jordan sighed.

"What's the matter, big man?" Crystal said.

"I hate my job," Jordan said. "I want to do something different with my life."

Crystal propped herself up on an elbow. "I've been waiting for you to say that!"

"You have?"

"You're too smart and cute to be a teacher."

"I just don't get it," he said. "On Earth, it's a noble profession, like being a doctor or a desalinization plant operator."

"In case you haven't noticed, this isn't Earth," she said. "Look, let's be honest, you and I both know that the schools here are a sham, that the MDC only operates them at the most basic levels because otherwise the Earth Council would hit us with crazy fines. All the good teachers went private years ago."

"But that's not fair. It's not just."

"It's not," she said. "I agree. Things should be a little more equal. But you're not going to change things working down there in the pit."

"But what else can I do?"

"Come work with me at the MDC," she said. "You're smart, you're adaptable, you're *adorable.* Change things from the top."

"But what can I do?"

"We'll put you through Leadership Camp," she said. "It'll get you physically and mentally ready."

"For what?"

She looked at him with pity in her eyes. "For war, silly," she said. "In case you hadn't realized it from all the explosions around. You know, like the one that killed my brother. We're not going to sit around and take it anymore. We're going to knock out the resistance."

"I don't know," Jordan said. "War is wrong in any context."

Crystal slinked up close to him. Her hand slid across his thigh, hitting pay dirt. There was still plenty of Mars Dust in Jordan's system. His wanker stood to attention like a cadet on graduation day.

"The war could use a stud like you," she said into his ear. Her tongue flicked across his lobe.

Jordan moaned.

Maybe he'd give war a try.

17

They stood at the edge of the habitable zone, amid the rubble of discarded billboards and artists' supplies. Sonia had grouped Leonard with two other trainees, a brother and sister who had recently realized that their jobs as soup strainers in the basement of an exclusive nightclub were not proper building blocks for a healthy and productive life. The resistance offered the only other alternative.

"Every week, more and more people are waking up," Sonia said. "The MDC can only maintain the illusion for so long. But we have to be prepared for whatever comes. And that includes the harsh Martian perma-winter. Are you prepared?"

"Sure!" Leonard exclaimed. He'd managed to score a Space Cake from one of the nurse assistants, and he was feeling good. The Martian gravitational system had caused him to lose body mass, and the drugs really went to his head.

The brother and sister, who had a firmer grip on what was really going on, nodded solemnly.

"Outside of this dome," Sonia said, "the temperature is negative seventy-six degrees Celsius. There is no breathable air. Let us have no illusions about the planet that we actually inhabit. This is not the MDC's party planet. It is a real place, a dead place, a place that belongs to the people."

Though the elite of Mars now had access to impermeable skin-hugging bodysuits that came complete with detachable wings for cliff soaring, the rest of Mars's population didn't have time or money to escape New Austin's neon penumbra. The resistance could only gain access to faulty equipment.

Leonard and his fellow trainees wore bulbous suits—stolen from the archives of a fashion museum—with thick glass helmets, standard issue forty years ago. The resistance had hackers who were able to keep the breathing and communications systems going, but that didn't keep the suits from being cumbersome and clumsy, not to mention hopelessly out of fashion. They also wore pressurized gravity boots, designed to keep your legs from freezing and snapping off below the knees instantly upon exposure.

Leonard popped open the visor of his helmet and swallowed a hundred milligrams of high-potency insta-THC. If he was going to go out onto the surface of Mars—the real surface, for the first time—he was going to do it superhigh. This was why Gaia had made weed in the first place.

"Now listen carefully," Sonia said. "We've used cutters to create a door. It's only large enough for you to crawl through, and it can only stay open for thirty seconds before the atmosphere inside the dome becomes corrupted. So get out there fast. Your mission—and it's very simple—is to survive for fifteen minutes. When that time's up, we'll open the door again, and you'll have thirty seconds to get back inside safely. If you miss that window, you'll have to wait another fifteen minutes."

"That doesn't sound so bad," Leonard said.

"Not everyone survives," Sonia said.

"Oh," said Leonard.

The THC had taken effect, and he probably felt less concerned than he should have. He was ready for whatever Mars would serve up to him, or so he thought. Sonia walked the three trainees over to the edge of the dome.

"On your hands and knees," she said.

They did as commanded.

"Crawl forward. Notice how nice and warm the ground is?"

They did.

"It's a lie. Artificial floor heat. If you don't stand up instantly after getting outside, you will be stuck to the ground and ripped apart by wind. I wouldn't advise it. And make sure your helmet doesn't hit the ground. One crack in the visor, and you're dead."

She reached for a slot in the dome.

"Go now," she said, and opened the door.

The brother and sister crawled forward frantically. Leonard followed. He turned around, looked at Sonia, grinned, and gave a thumbs-up. She booted him in the ass, and he stumbled out.

Leonard stood immediately. The second he did, a gust of wind, stronger than anything he'd ever felt, blew him backward. He managed to right himself, his right boot skidding. Looking around, he saw pure desolation, nothing but vast red desert toward every horizon, a dead, freezing hellscape that couldn't have been imagined even in the most feverish moments of human desperation.

"Cool!" he said to himself.

He turned around. The brother had been blown against a rock formation. He lay on the ground, his suit punctured, writhing and twisting around like a balloon that had just been untied, doing a spastic, wormlike death dance. His sister stood above him, flapping her arms, clutching her helmet, screaming. She saw Leonard and waved him over.

Leonard started walking, but a gust blew him back. He tripped and went sprawling.

But his suit appeared to have held. Again the winds howled, in all directions at once. A sheet of bone-dry sand skittered across Leonard's visor. Even through his heavily insulated suit, he could feel the atmosphere freezing his bones. He looked back over to the brother and sister. The boy lay lifeless now, his body decaying rapidly. His sister was on her knees, head in hands. Leonard needed to get over to her.

There was a break in the wind. It only blew at near-tornado strength now. His boots were heavy. He lumbered across the blasted landscape like a beast of labor. It took him five minutes to travel a hundred feet. He could see the body of the boy freezing. He would crack apart at the touch, just like that. Something vile rose in Leonard's throat, but he choked it back down. The girl wasn't moving. Her eyes lifted to him, searching and desperate, yellow in her visor's sick glow. Leonard gestured for her to come with him. She didn't move. He gestured again. She wept copiously in her helmet. He lifted her by her armpits. Her body went slack, as they'd been taught in protest training. She wanted to die out here. He wasn't going to let her.

Her boots dragged along the ground as Leonard moved her, far too slowly, her weight twice what it normally would have been. Leonard wasn't that strong, he wasn't that fit, and he wasn't that brave. But he still wanted to save her.

The door opened. He had thirty seconds. Leonard grunted. He could feel sweat freezing on his body, the suit operating at the very edge of its effectiveness. He pulled the girl, who seemed to have fainted. No exhortations were going to get her moving. With ten seconds left, he reached the door, turned around, and, with a tremendous heave, stuffed her through, feetfirst.

The door closed. Leonard was alone. He'd been on the surface for fifteen minutes and had explored approximately one-eighth of a mile. One of his companions was dead, one had almost died, and now he was probably going to die as well. A huge, swirling cone of dust moved toward him. The exertion had depleted his oxygen reserves, and he was already gulping for breath. Leonard shielded his eyes and prepared to be blown into oblivion. This was it.

Behind and below him, the door snapped open. Sonia came out, fully suited. Her strong hands grabbed his shoulders and dragged him backward through the door.

"Get in here, you idiot," Sonia said.

He took off his helmet. His breath came in gulps.

"I thought I had to wait another fifteen minutes," he said.

"Sometimes," she said, "we'll make exceptions."

"For what?"

"For exceptional people."

"I'm not exceptional."

"That was a heroic act out there," she said. "The resistance needs you."

"I need some drugs. Right now."

"Hah!" she said. "I bet you do." So she gave him some, and said, "Time for you to meet Captain Ted."

♦ ♦ ♦

Captain Ted lived alone on the twenty-third floor of an abandoned high-rise, surrounded by memories. These mostly were comprised of holographic snapshots of him living on the streets of New Austin as a younger man, strung out on injectable Mars Dust. There were also several coffee-table books of graffiti art installations that had long since been painted over. He kept them in books because books are sacred and must be preserved forever.

"Back then, art was real," he was saying, while horking weed vapor out of a plastic bag. "It was something you could stick your dick into. Everyone was poor, everything was shitty, you could get murdered on a hover-train for a dollar. I had a friend who put nails through her palms. On stage. In front of an audience. Every week for a year. To prove a point. And she loved it, right?"

He passed the vapo-bag to Leonard, who took a grateful puff.

"Definitely," Leonard said.

Captain Ted was wearing a vintage Intergalactic Policeman hat, as well as matching work boots. To him, this was an ironic commentary on the wretched state of the workingman in outer space. He had a curlicued mustache, dyed black. As he twirled its ends, Sonia, who was sitting next to Leonard on a wretched, worn-out sofa, beamed with admiration.

"What Captain Ted is saying is that things used to be better on Mars," she said. "Life was *real.* It was authentic. You could feel the vibrations of the planet underneath you."

"Yeah, man," Captain Ted said. "That's why I started this revolution. To bring back the real."

To bring back the past, Leonard thought. *When you were young.* But he didn't say that.

"Captain Ted is the inspiration for us all," said Sonia.

"When I see the people out there in open rebellion against the system," Captain Ted said, "it makes me feel warm inside. Fuck the MDC and its goddamn piggy fascism. The land belongs to the people. There's more to life than watching other people wait in line to eat at restaurants."

"Tell Leonard what happened," Sonia said. "Tell him *why* you started the revolution."

"We were living in a commune," Ted said. "It was not-for-profit. It was about the arts. And free love, of course, but mostly it was about making things. Music. Art. Interactive poetry holograms. Space Kabuki. We had this band called Willful Children; we played seventy-two-hour concerts without stopping. The *New Austinist,* before it sold out and became an MDC-humping rag, called us 'the first band to capture the cry of the authentic Mars from its withered soul.' I remember that quote because it's true, you know?"

"Sure," Leonard said.

"Anyway, we had this festival, really free—well, mostly free. It was like five dollars to get in so, you know, we could afford food and water, but you got to stay all week if you wanted to. We called it Mars by Mars, because, you know, Mars used to be authentically genuine. There were restaurants that stayed open all day and never had any customers—on purpose. You could sit in the ditch and play ukulele and someone would make a movie about you. We had a thing we called Flying Tits Week, where everyone would like make these fake-tit drones and fly them around. The sky was full of winged boobies. There was one guy. He used to ride around naked on a unicycle. *And nobody cared.* That's what Mars was all about."

"So, let me guess," Leonard said. "The MDC police force came in and busted up the festival, maybe even killed a couple of people."

"No, man," said Captain Ted. "Way worse. They *stole our name.*"

"What?"

"Yeah, they saw that the festival was called Mars by Mars, so they started their own, with the same name. We hadn't thought about protecting the name because, you know, art belongs to the people. Honestly, we didn't think anyone was interested.

"But then they started doing their own festival. It was really slick, had all these rules, you had to apply to participate, and, whatever, we did ours at the same time. But they had all the money and the power, and eventually, people stopped going to us and started going to them. But not because they were better. It's because the people *changed*, man. They were *brainwashed* by the corporate holograms. The MDC took away our art, they took away our houses, they took away our streets. *They brought in bands from Earth.* Fuck that. Everyone knows Earth music sucks. So we went *underground*. We decided to fight."

"That's what this is about?" Leonard said. "A trademark dispute? And you react by setting off bombs in nightclubs and killing innocent people? Seems a little extreme."

Captain Ted put down the vapo-bag and looked at Leonard seriously, as though he were a scientist studying a fresh soil sample from an unexplored planet.

"Are you callin' bullshit on me?" he said.

Leonard shrugged. Captain Ted laughed, a great big vapor throat of a laugh.

"Ha-ha-ha-ha-ha-ha-ha!" he howled, throwing his head up to the sky. "Ha-ha-ha-ha-ha! Sonia, I like this one! It's been years since anyone called bullshit on me. That's the problem with this revolution! Too many yes-men."

The old coot looked at Leonard straight on and said, "This is why we need you, kid. Because you tell the truth. You see things with an outside perspective. You're not all worn down and cynical from a dozen winters on the edge of the wasteland. That's what Keeping Mars Weird is all about. Telling the truth and not caring about consequences. That is art. That is revolution."

With that pronouncement, Captain Ted's head lolled back. He snored.

"Sometimes that happens when his brain works too hard," Sonia said. "He thinks more than all of us put together."

Captain Ted snorted awake: "And another thing!" he said.

With that, Leonard Tolliver realized that he had somehow accidentally become the pawn of a Martian revolutionary army run by a half-senile art crank. It wasn't what he'd expected when he'd come to Mars, but it was still pretty interesting. Leonard hoped things were going just as well for Jordan.

Wherever he was.

18

Jordan Kincaid snapped awake, gasping for air. Sweat sheened across every pore. He looked around. He was in a room, bare except for recessed ceiling lighting, with brushed-steel walls and a black window off to his left. To his right was some sort of platform with little levels and dials and needles on it. He was strapped to a table.

His arms slid out of the straps without a problem. Whatever the straps were for, they weren't meant to keep him prisoner. He looked at his arm. His muscles were taut and defined, which surprised him because he'd been a withered, wasted wreck since he'd arrived on Mars. His head felt . . . clear. He could actually think.

A recessed panel in the wall opened. In came Crystal Waters, wearing a very fetching, low-cut lab coat.

"Ah, good," she said. "You're awake."

"Where am I, Crystal?"

"You're at MDC Executive Training headquarters," she said. "Don't worry, you don't have anything to fear. This is all part of the program."

"What program?"

"We've identified you for a leadership role in the MDC's ongoing efforts."

"To do what?"

Crystal pecked him on the cheek. "To run Mars, silly," she said. "We need people like you. Most people from Earth who come to Mars are too exhausted from working to do anything, and we all know the Martian education system produces nothing but trendy morons. You have the perfect combination of an elite background, youth, and"—she looked him up and down—"a hard body that can take punishment."

Jordan licked his lips. "I'm thirsty."

"I bet you are, space cowboy," she said. "Detox can really drain a man."

"What do you mean, detox?"

"You had enough Mars Dust in your bloodstream to permanently stun a horse," she said. "Now, that's what we want for most of the population, but leadership needs a clean mind. You should only snort the dust selectively, like before sex or maybe the occasional concert. So we put you through training."

Jordan looked at her quizzically.

"Oh, right, you wouldn't remember. Basically, to speed up the process, we feed you vitamin-formula discs that enhance your body's functioning on Mars, without all the usual depletion that comes with interplanetary travel. All MDC employees get it. That's how we keep our edge. The resistance has to constantly exercise and steal food in order to just *maintain*, whereas we gradually improve."

A lab technician entered the room, pushing a cart. He pulled away a sheet, revealing a sumptuous buffet of water and juice and breads and fruits and meats and cheeses. Jordan slipped the rest of his restraints and popped onto the floor, feeling surprisingly steady.

"I haven't had balance like this since I was on Earth," he said.

"That's exactly the point," said Crystal, running her finger down his chest. "We keep you in optimum condition so you can be useful to us."

Jordan could wait no longer. He lifted up the pitcher of cool, clear, filtered water and gulped it greedily, precious rivulets splashing all along his muscular chest and arms. Crystal ran her tongue over her teeth lasciviously.

"My juices run sweet," she said.

The door whooshed open. Dick Waters, looking splendidly robust thanks to all manner of padding and false skin, strode into the room.

"Cut it out, Crystal," he said. "You'd think you'd never gotten laid before."

"Just trying to be a good hostess, Daddy."

"Save it for later," said Waters. "Let me have a look at our new specimen. Hello, Kincaid."

Jordan looked up from his feast. He had a mouthful of cheese. "Mmph," he said.

"Feeling better, are we?"

Jordan swallowed, then took a gulp of water. "Yes, sir," he said. "I feel fantastic."

"I want you to look at this footage," Waters said.

He waved his hand, and 3-D footage appeared on the platform next to Jordan's gurney. Jordan was emaciated, huddled in the corner, shivering. Two men came into the room and injected something into his arm. Jordan was too weak to fight them. "Get away from me," he moaned. "*Auuuuugh*! The flies! The flies! Make them stop! *Please!*"

"Wow," Jordan said. "I don't remember any of that."

"This is what happens when someone tries to kick Mars Dust without our help," Waters said. "Which is why everyone on this planet is hopped up all the time. We supply our vitamin-supplement discs selectively, to worthy candidates."

"I don't know what to say," Jordan said.

Waters snapped his fingers, and a flunky rolled in a chair. Waters sat down. "You'll thank me when we've got this fucking planet restored to normal and we can bring this stupid resistance to its knees. Do you have any idea what this planet was *like* before the MDC got here?"

Jordan shook his head. "Nope," he said.

"It was a *shit-hole*, that's what it was like," said Waters. "Everything was *filthy*. The city had completely decayed. People lived in houses without roofs. They had to. One out of every three didn't have a job, and those who worked didn't make much. People shot one another. In the streets. Over bread. I saw kids playing in open sewers. I saw pregnant women eating garbage to survive. I once saw someone gunned down on a spaceport shuttle because he'd offered a blowjob to another trick's regular customer. *This* is what the resistance wants back. This is the old New Austin that they're so nostalgic for. Sure, there used to be a lot of public murals, and there were some really good bands. I went to some concerts, I had fun, and I got fucked up. I was young once, too. But is a small avant-garde art scene from three decades ago that barely anybody participated in, even when it was happening, really the basis for a sound urban-development policy?"

"No?" Jordan guessed. He didn't know exactly what to say, mostly because he had no idea what Waters was talking about. But he did know that the MDC had fed him and brought him back to health. His mother had always told him to butter the egos of the people who buttered your bread. Even if those egos had clearly become unhinged.

"We set it all straight," Waters said. "We showed them. Sure, there's a lot of traffic now, and housing prices are pretty high, but come on! Can you *possibly* tell me that what's going on now is worse?"

"No," Jordan said, without the question mark this time. Waters was really rolling now.

"Right answer. No. It's not. You legalize drugs, encourage entrepreneurship, and remove all zoning restrictions. *That's* how you make things better. And it is better. Way better. So much fucking better that I just want to *kill* all those resistance people. Kill them where they sleep."

"Calm down, Daddy," Crystal said. "You'll make your perma-skin itch."

"Of course, of course," Waters said. "I just get so angry. They did kill my only son, misbegotten as he was."

"Poor David," said Crystal. "He just wanted to party."

Waters stood up and slapped Jordan on the back. "But we have a pretty good replacement for him with Kincaid, here, I'd say!"

This made Jordan very uncomfortable. If he was really David's replacement, then he'd been committing some very incestuous acts with Crystal. Still, he had to roll forward.

"Are you ready to join the MDC team, Jordan?" Waters asked.

"Absolutely, sir," Jordan said.

"Good."

Waters spoke into his wrist. "Bring in the prisoner," he said.

The door whooshed open. In came two guards, holding a wretched-looking, manacled, bearded man, maybe Jordan's age, maybe younger, clad in rags. He stank of filth. His arms and legs were nothing but bone.

The man still struggled a little, but he was so weak the guards had no trouble strapping him on to the table Jordan had just vacated.

"Fuck you, fascist," the man said to Waters.

"Ah, see, this is what the resistance thinks of our efforts to make Mars a better place," said Waters. "They spit on us and call us political names that they don't understand. It's that kind of confusion that leads them to murder our sons and daughters in the name of a cause that they're too stupid to actually understand."

He leaned into the young man's face. "Isn't that right, dummy?"

The young man spat. A fat gob caught Waters right between the eyes. Waters crinkled his fake nose and wiped it with a kerchief.

"And there you go," he said. "Jordan, would you do the honors?"

"What honors?"

"Of showing our guest how we deal with rude behavior."

Waters nodded to the guards, one of whom handed Jordan an extra-large double-barreled pellet gun. Jordan looked at Crystal. She nodded at him. It was apparent what they wanted him to do.

Jordan assessed his situation. On the one hand, murder was an unspeakable crime, committed only by Earth's most depraved and insane inhabitants. On the other, he had his future to consider—his material future, his professional future, his sexual future, and probably all kinds of other futures that he'd yet to imagine.

"And what happens if I don't do the honors?" Jordan said.

"Then we'll consider your training a failure," said Waters. "And we'll have to start over. From the beginning."

Jordan raised the gun, pulled the trigger, and blew a bowling-ball-sized hole through the terrified man's chest.

Dick Waters looked pleased. "He's an ice-cold killer," he said. "Just like his father."

19

Sonia Smartphone had a first-class hover-pedi license, like a lot of members of the resistance. There were a number of reasons why she needed one. Not only was the money pretty good—particularly if you had free public housing—but it also provided great intel. Only rich people used the upper lanes. When Sonia got them in her cab, they were often drunk and babbling. Some of the resistance's greatest bombing targets had come from hover-pedi spying. That was how they'd known how to get David Waters and how they'd assassinated Dick Waters's second wife at her birthday party. Sonia had ferreted out both locations.

She kept her doings subtle, and that made her the best. In general, the resistance tried to blend in. Anonymity was important. They wore ordinary workers' clothing and, with few exceptions, eschewed showy tattoos or odd hairstyles while adopting common names and taking normal jobs. Captain Ted told them never to express anything radical in public. Even the most basic critiques of society, other than the obvious "Oh my Gaia, this restaurant line is *too* long," needed to remain unsaid.

Sonia Smartphone—her name derived from a strange late twenty-first-century nostalgia trend that caused a quarter of the human population to legally change their patronymics to the names of outdated tech products—whizzed along the upper lanes on her hover-pedi, relatively unfettered. It was only livery drivers up here. The noise and mess of the city lurched forty feet below, while the stratospheric hover-sports hobbyists whizzed forty feet above.

Summoning a pedi was such a simple system, relatively unchanged in the last five centuries. If Sonia became available, she'd get a ping on her Device, fly over to a prearranged stand—a private entrance behind a club or restaurant or luxury tower—hover down, pick up the passengers, and zoom away to an already-logged address. Words were very rarely exchanged, and credits were transferred automatically. It was the most ingenious system ever devised to keep social classes separate.

She turned off the meter and dropped down a few feet, to the very limit of legal, and observed the street scene below. The people of New Austin, slaves to their fashion apps, always wore something different. Today, it was puffy green pantaloons and sleeveless yellow T-shirts depicting the cartoon character Hungry Horse snorting Mars Dust out of a picnic basket. This had been the trend lately. Restaurants and clubs threw "party picnics," changing their décor inside to match. The better-funded ones actually created artificial picnic grounds, with actual grass and picnic tables inside, serving sandwiches, chips, artisanal pop, and Space Cakes laced with high-end Mars Dust. It would be all the rage for the next few weeks.

But no matter the trend du jour, Sonia observed the changing details from above, unmoved. The relentless novelty couldn't mask a crushing sameness. Who were these people? Where did they come from? How did they live? Sonia had no idea. She survived because she lived in a secret anarchist megacommune located in an abandoned public-housing tower. Everyone else just seemed to appear on the street, and they were strange to her.

All anyone ever did in New Austin was wait in line for restaurants that they didn't like and then return to substandard housing that they couldn't afford.

It hadn't always been like that.

Sonia had been born on Mars and had grown up in the same house that her father had been born in. It was, her father said, a "real Martian house," hand-hewn of naturally insulated Martian stone, reinforced by beams of rot-proof Earth wood that her grandfather had worked thirty years to obtain. She was a fourth-generation Martian and was Martian proud. Her homestead had been only seven hundred square feet, but it was efficiently organized, with working plumbing, a state-supplied food printer, and plenty of storage space, as well as a rear-plot vegetable garden. In those days, there were about a million Martians. Most of them had Enough.

Her father worked hard sometimes but not much at all other times. Many of her fondest memories involved sitting around the wintertime peat hearth, playing with her Device while her father smoked grass and practiced his guitar and her mother weaved physics equations with her macramé set. Everyone was educated in the old times.

They lived on what was then the outskirts of downtown. When they ventured into the city, to run errands or to see the Kabuki circus, they could see how dirty and rundown and dangerous it had become. But life was comfortable in their particular patch. They were space bohemians of the highest order.

Then President Reginald Patel, known throughout the galaxy as "The Development Killer," died halfway through his sixth term. His populist successors were weak, with no stomach for a real fight. The MDC moved into the breach. They infiltrated the cops, shut down hop dens and gig halls, and filled the jails with freaks and junkies. And they started buying up property. One day a gigantic starship arrived on Mars containing forty-five hydrogen-fuel-cell megadozers. They didn't stop working.

Even as the neighborhood mutated around them, Sonia's parents didn't want to sell the homestead. They fought every property-tax increase and zoning restriction. Every other single-family home was either torn down for condos or turned into an expensive vacation rental. A bistro selling "food inspired by the spices of Mercury" opened across the street next door to a hot-yoga studio. Still, they held their ground.

One night when Sonia was about ten years old, her father's Device vibrated. He looked at it.

"Shit," he said.

"What?" said Sonia's mother.

"They charged us a life's fortune back property tax."

"It must be a mistake. We're completely up to date on all our taxes. This property was paid for decades ago!"

"There's been a reassessment."

"They can't do that!"

"They can do whatever they want," he said solemnly.

A week later, a megadozer appeared across the street. There was a knock at the door.

Sonia's dad answered. An agent wearing the silver unitard of the MDC Corps was standing there, looking solemn.

"Stuart Smartphone?" he said.

"Yes," said Sonia's dad.

The functionary read from his Device. "I have an order from the Martian Development Corporation to demolish your home," he said. "You have forfeited your right to this property by authority of section 17.3 of the Martian Development Corporation Code. Despite repeated warnings—"

"Repeated warnings!" Sonia's mother shouted from the inside. "You just informed us about this a week ago. You can't—"

"Despite repeated warnings," the functionary continued, "you have not responded. You have one hour to vacate your home willingly, or be forcibly removed by MDC personnel. We have arranged for temporary housing in Dormitory Village by the spaceport, until such time as when your credit has sufficiently recovered to purchase—"

Sonia's father held up a hand. "I get it," he said. "Let me meet with my family."

The functionary nodded. Sonia's father closed the door and turned to face his wife and only daughter.

"They've got us," he said.

Both Sonia and her mother were blubbering.

"Don't be afraid," he said. "And don't cry."

He turned to Sonia. "You have to be tougher than they are," he said. "Until they are gone." And then he turned to his wife. "I need you both to go outside, across the street."

She looked at him pleadingly. "Don't—"

"We talked about this," he said. "We knew it was going to happen."

So Sonia's mother took Sonia across the street, through the drought-resistant front lawn she'd spent so many years cultivating, and the gate that she and her husband had made by hand, and all the semi-ironic metal sculptures of frogs playing in a rock band. She walked across the street, turning to face the little red-soil structure, painted a deep purple, that was the only true home she'd ever known. And she turned on her Device to stream. Everyone had to see what was about to happen.

Sonia's father appeared at the upstairs window, armed with buckshot. He fired, hitting the functionary smack in the face, blowing off the top of his head. Three seconds later, the megadozer whirred, shot a beam, surrounded the house in a bright blue glow, and then, with a high-pitched noise and then a puff, vaporized it into oblivion. Sonia screamed as her entire life turned to ash before her eyes.

Sonia's mother screamed, and everyone on Mars saw what had happened.

The resistance started that day.

No one was surprised when Sonia joined.

♦ ♦ ♦

Now she hovered near where her home had once stood. Only three buildings remained from Sonia's childhood, two of them restaurant storefronts operated by organized criminals, and one a legendary Martian dancehall that the MDC had been unsuccessful in removing from the historic register. All were surrounded by massive condominium developments with trendy Venusian coffeehouses on their ground floors (Venus's coffee was the best because it was "hot roasted"). Her former home turf had become the most exclusive neighborhood in all New Austin, a place that adopted trends *days* before anyone else. All the best picnics went down here.

Sonia's Device sounded. "Two VIPs at Knife+Feather waiting for pickup," it said.

Knife+Feather was a private dining room within a club within a club. It accepted no reservations, and you couldn't wait in line to get in. No one was allowed to review it, and the menu remained secret. This could be a juicy fare. It might pay for up to three guns on the black market.

Sonia hovered down and waited in the queue. Her clients appeared: an impossibly elegant woman in a sleek white jumpsuit and matching broad-rimmed hat and scarf, and a stunningly handsome man with a near-perfect physique that made his classical tuxedo look like body armor. Maybe it even *was* body armor. Sonia got excited. These weren't ordinary trendoids. She'd stumbled into some ruling-class fish.

They moved languidly into the backseat. Sonia raised the barrier. They clearly wanted privacy. She could give them the illusion of it. There was a microphone embedded into the rear cushion, and a disposable filmstrip along the doorframe. Sonia hit "Record" on her Device.

"Oh, Jordan," the woman said. "What a lovely picnic!"

The man barely grunted.

"It's been so long since I've tasted Earth meat. Except for *yours*," she said.

Sonia winced. Nothing disgusted her more than rich people getting it on. As with everything else, they acted like they were *entitled* to sex, and they talked about it in the most vulgar way.

"I can't wait to get home and see your—your *arms*. They have gotten so huge."

The man grunted again, this time in a pleased sort of way. Sonia lifted off, and the hover-pedi carried them toward the preset destination. "Waters Plaza—Penthouse," the display read.

Only one person lived in the penthouse of Waters Plaza: Crystal Waters, the heir to the throne, the richest woman on Mars, the scourge of the slums. She was slumming, as she was famous for doing. Crystal of course had access to as many private vehicles as she wanted, but she also occasionally liked to be "among the people," at least in her mind. It usually just meant taking a public taxi home from a private restaurant.

I should just turn around right now and blow both their heads off, Sonia Smartphone thought.

It would be quick and easy, a huge propaganda victory for the people. But she thought three to four moves ahead, as Captain Ted had taught her over endless games of Punk Chess, which he made her play with him for hours. And four moves down the road, she knew that the MDC would trace the movements of Sonia's hover-pedi to the garage and then would follow its time-stamp back to the projects, and then the movement would be vaporized.

"You've just gotten so *strong*," Crystal Waters said.

"Have I?"

This was why Sonia trolled the after-midnight shift. No one would ever give away the location of a top-secret corporate motivational expedition during work hours. And the woman just kept talking. It was better to listen than to kill.

"I can't wait to fuck you in the Traveldome," Crystal said.

Traveldome? Sonia thought.

"Mr. Chief of Security for the Summit Summit," said Crystal. "Big job for a big man. Are you proud?"

"Yeah," Jordan said.

"You should be," said Crystal. "A week from tonight, at the Southeast Gate you're all mine."

"I'm always all yours," Jordan said.

"Are you going to fuck me on Olympus Mons?"

"Sure."

From there, it was all snuffling and grunting, so Sonia shut off the feed, knowing that her loathsome fares had begun their predictable post-picnic, post–Mars Dust dessert snog.

Five minutes later, Sonia's hover-pedi arrived at the dock for Waters Tower. Her fares stumbled out of the back without even looking at her, their hands halfway down each other's pants. What did they care? The first lady of Mars could do whatever she wanted, and if anyone dared question it, they'd be killed.

Sonia's Device pinged. They had only left her a 10 percent tip.

Goddamn cheap-ass rich bastards, she thought.

They deserved to die.

Soon, they would.

Sonia clocked off her hover-pedi and her Device, and lowered down to the regular driving lanes, which at this time of night didn't have too many delays but were still crowded enough to keep her anonymous.

Wheeling around the restaurant district, which was always crowded, no matter the time of day, she skirted the financial center and then headed out toward the spaceport, where she got the hover-pedi up to a hundred kilometers per hour, the maximum planetary speed allowed by the Galactic Travel Council.

Turning left, she went over the soybean plantations and milk dispensaries, which, she noted, were slowly beginning to disappear, replaced by sketchy-looking houses and cheap storefronts. Nothing stayed the same. Everything changed.

Change was bad.

Change had to die.

Finally, after she'd done a near-complete loop around all of New Austin, she slipped through the historic district, where the really old Martian money sat buried somewhere inside the "traditional" four-thousand-square-foot adobe mounds, and headed back through the trend district, where the newly arrived, newly wealthy, or always stupid ate and did whatever their Devices told them to. Sonia cruised through a few blocks peppered with Earth trees that were actually kind of quiet and pleasant, and, finally, into the neighborhood right next to where she'd originally picked up the fare, which wasn't quite as trendy as the trend district but was going to be pretty soon. Rents were rising fast.

She pulled up in front of the Black Pig. It was rolling, even this time of night. From all the hover-pedis parked outside, she could see that the resistance had gathered at its favorite spot, the oldest bar on Mars, the place where Johnny and the Waffles had done that recording of "Fuck the MDC" that had gone so viral and made so much money that even Dick Waters couldn't ban it. The profits had allowed Johnny to buy the land, to admit anyone he wanted at any time, ID free, and, most importantly, had won him a fifty-year amnesty from MDC inspection and Device monitoring, which was usually mandatory.

The place offered safe harbor for the resistance, and it was a glorious shit-hole.

Sonia walked into the dank chamber full of drunken revolutionaries and hack poets. Enormous steam valves in the sidewalls were constantly releasing a thick mist, giving the bar the aura of a forgotten sewer. Its walls were covered with the graffiti tags of punks long dead, the tables carved with the slashings of a thousand pocketknives. From the ceiling hung bras and panties and jockstraps and toupees, the relics of lost dares, as well as a plaster cast of the Earth, pierced through the center by a sword, dripping blood.

"Fuck the MDC" played over the system, as usual. Sonia was actually kind of tired of the song, which she'd never admit in revolutionary company. It got people so hyped, even after all these years.

Fuck the MDC.
Fuck the MDC.
They've fucked you and me.
Fuck the MDC.

It went on like that, boringly. But the people were angry. They didn't have access to a lot of good equipment, and they were poorly educated. This led to simple three-chord songs.

Sonia saw Leonard Tolliver at the bar. Leonard hadn't proven himself again since that heroic day outside the dome, and he hadn't been that good in the training. On the other hand, he had mastered doing shots with his dorm-mates. It led Sonia to wonder if she'd misread him.

Leonard nodded and smiled, always friendly. "Hey, dude!" he said. "Long live the revolution!"

"Right, right," said Sonia. "Have you seen the captain?"

Leonard looked upward. "I think he's holding court in his loft."

Captain Ted had a little room above the bar where he liked to sit at night, smoking weed and talking about the days when Mars was young and the streets had flowed with glorious shit. He was in there now, with an audience of a half dozen rapturous young revolutionaries.

"We had this night," Sonia heard him saying as she climbed the stairs, "every week, where we'd reenact movies, like old ones from the twenty-first century, except we'd do it naked, with a dominatrix whipping us for hours. They were *marathons.* And people would watch, and watch, and watch—let me tell you, the drugs were *pure* then. Real Mars Dust, distilled into liquid form, shot through the veins with a—" He saw Sonia top the stairs. "Look at that," he said. "Lieutenant Smartphone, fresh from patrol. What's the word from the cold, cruel city?"

"I hooked the big fish," Sonia said.

"Oh-ho!" said Captain Ted.

"Seriously, man," she said. "How many Sherpas have we got?"

20

Jordan Kincaid walked through an alley, armored. Breathable, flexible, state-of-the-art gear covered every inch of his body. An elite guard needed to be able to deflect cannon fire while also executing a drop-and-roll or a proper fence dive.

Around his belt, Jordan had more weapons than the ancient Earth hero, Batman: stun pistols, smoke grenades, throwing stars, knives—an endless array of implements designed to maim and kill anarchists. Actually, they could kill anyone, but the MDC used them on anarchists mostly.

Jordan moved carefully along the edges, seeking the shadows.

It was night, somewhere between 1:00 and 4:00 a.m., but the interior of the New Austin dome glowed more brightly than it did during the day because of all the nightlife, which really didn't get started until midnight because that's when people finally got done waiting in line for dinner. This created a strange optical environment where you could move from flickering shadow to blinding argon glow to pitch blackness, all within seconds. Jordan had his goggles set to auto-adjust accordingly.

The sky whirled with hover-pedis and trucks making their late-night vodka powder and Mars Dust deliveries. Digital ads appeared and disappeared in the skies at random. Overflowing bowls of ramen slurped by cartoon characters had replaced the wonders of the Milky Way in the night sky. The people were happy with that.

Jordan heard some noise from behind a Dumpster across the alley and dropped to a crouch, moving close to the wall. Those punks could be anywhere.

He moved slowly, serpentinely. A brick exploded over his head. Jordan kept his cool, pivoted, whipped around the corner, and hit the deck, splat into a fetid puddle from his waist to his elbows. That was the least of his problems. He turned his visor upward. He could see one of those arrogant resistance fuckers up in the window across the way, his face low, searching the alley with a laser-scoped rifle. The little red dot marking the source of the laser shifted subtly toward his position, but Jordan followed it calmly with his eyes, which had been fitted with lasers of their own.

Jordan took a fissionated pea gun out of his weapons belt. It had at least a half dozen pellets loaded. He'd only need one, maybe two. Jordan put the pea gun to his lips, tilted his head slightly upward, and let out two tiny puffs of air, his head nudging slightly to the right for the second one.

The window above the anarchist exploded. The anarchist looked slightly surprised, a reaction that he was allowed to have for half a second, before the second pellet buried itself between his eyes. He slumped forward, dead, his rifle clanging onto the fire escape below.

One down. Jordan flipped up to his feet, then tumbled behind the Dumpster, knife drawn. There he met a surprised-looking rebel, whom he slit from belly to chops. He stood up and mentally commanded his visor to infrared.

The doorways and windows and corners of the alley bloomed with little blobs of heat. It was a damn ambush! Jordan had been in worse, though. The brick above his head exploded. He turned, his suit instantly calculating the angle from which it had been fired, and caught a guy in the chest. From there, it was cherry-picking. Jordan whirled around like a turret, missing three out of every four shots, because precision wasn't his goal. Spraying was the best way to eradicate pests.

Suddenly the alley was quiet. Jordan scanned around. All the heat blobs had gone blue, except for one, which was slowly slinking its way along the ground toward the end of the alley. Jordan adjusted his visor to normal view and walked over. A blubbering anarchist, lightly wounded, was trying to get out of the alley alive, the sucker.

Jordan was on him in seconds, rolling him over. The anarchist had his feet and hands in the air, twitching like a bug.

"Please!" he said. "I have kids."

"You should have thought of that before you fucked with the MDC," Jordan said. "Now who sent you here, and where is your hideout?"

"I can't tell you that," the anarchist squealed through his sad little beard-framed mouth.

"Are you *sure*?"

"I'm sure!"

Jordan lifted his boot over the man's head. The man screamed. Jordan stamped down.

The lights came on. The door to the simulator room opened, and Dick and Crystal Waters stepped through it.

"I *told* you he was ready, Daddy dear," Crystal said. "No one has taken to the training quite like Jordan." She walked over to him and removed his helmet. "He's very . . . suggestible."

Jordan stood stoically. Dick Waters walked over and examined him like a particularly delicious artisanal salami. He ran a finger over Jordan's chest, his false teeth gleaming in the fluorescence.

"It was definitely an impressive display," Waters said. "I'll be in good hands on the mountain. Crystal has explained to you what this is going to be, right, Kincaid?"

"Only that it's important," Jordan said.

"Well, I don't know about that. But it's important to me, and that's what matters, right?"

"Yes, sir."

"I conceived of the Summit Summit as a way to really bring Mars together. It's the only way all the Device developers and writers and artists that I admire can have a chance to talk to the people who really make Mars tick—the businesspeople—without having to hustle. We want to help them, and they want to help us, and that's what makes Mars tick. I'm all about the free exchange of ideas. That's why we have so many cultural festivals. Many of which get dreamed up at the Summit Summit. It keeps the Mars brand alive. Does that make sense, Kincaid?"

"Of course it does, sir."

"You *are* well trained!" Waters said delightedly. "I'm just bullshitting, of course; it's really a chance to get drunk and wasted and eat rich food and fuck, on a mountain. But sometimes we have conversations, too."

"Sounds good, sir."

"Got to give the people something to look up to!"

"Daddy," Crystal said, "quit babbling. Jordan has got to be tired after that exhausting training session."

"I'm fine," Jordan said.

"Of *course* that's what you'd say," said Crystal. She pulled a clear disc from her pocket. "Here you go, you poor dear; it's time for your wafer."

Jordan opened his mouth. She put it on his tongue. Within seconds, his body relaxed, his cortisol levels returning to normal and then dropping below normal. For hours, he'd been hyperalert, and suddenly he was a drooling wreck.

"You sure you can control this one?" Dick Waters said.

"I've got him, Daddy," Crystal said. "Don't worry."

♦ ♦ ♦

From the luxury rooftop prison where Crystal kept him, Jordan could see the entire New Austin skyline. It glittered with a low-burn luminescence, infinite power drawn from an infinite-enough life force—the sun—that moved everything in the city, from the coffee generators to the hover-pedis. Before, Crystal had told him, the city lacked power half the time. They were sucking fuel from the Martian core, which was causing sinkholes. And now look at it, the shining, domed jewel of the universe.

He took a sip of his cucumber-infused PowerWater—a finely tuned formula to induce maximum muscle growth and political apathy—and sighed. This is what it had come to: an elite megasuite with unlimited maid and food service. All they asked for in return was his integrity. And his body. And his spirit.

Jordan had his shirt off. He looked at himself in the glass and didn't recognize what was looking back. He'd come to Mars a little idealistic, a little confused, and maybe a little weak. It's not that he didn't remember who and what he was before; it was that he didn't care. The "vitamins" had sapped him of nostalgia and all but a shred of empathy. Sure, the MDC still needed him smart; an education like Jordan's, solid and diverse even by Earth's terms, made him an enormous asset on Mars. The native-born knew nothing, by design. The immigrant population was made up of either trend-seeking, rich Earth dunderheads or indentured servants from Luna. Brains were in short supply.

Jordan was still confused about how the MDC used what little brainpower it had. He'd come to Mars to teach, albeit against his will. They'd deliberately stuck him in a third-rate facility and forced him to read moronic scripts to drooling automatons. But they'd also invested seemingly countless amounts of money into training and conditioning him into an efficient superspy killer. It was a direct reversal of his former priorities.

Still, of all the possible outcomes of Jordan's arrival on Mars, "soulless killing machine and sex puppet to the powerful" hadn't really been high on the agenda.

The door whooshed open.

Crystal walked in. "How is my noble warrior?" she said.

Jordan sat on the edge of his perfectly made bed. "Why am I doing this, Crystal?"

"Doing what, dear?" she said.

"I'm a teacher, not a soldier."

"Oh." Crystal sat down next to him. "Tell me what's wrong."

"I didn't even want to come to Mars in the first place," said Jordan, "and the moment I got here, my friend was killed, and then the job was terrible, and then . . . I'm not a killer, Crystal."

"We're not asking you to be a killer. We're asking you to *protect*, not destroy. And occasionally protectors have to kill. Very occasionally. "

"But these simulations—"

"Do you think the MDC *wants* New Austin to be like this? We're not the ones setting off dirty bombs at communal restaurants and staging anarchist dance-ins in office plazas. These people are living in the past, and they are killing innocents in the process. We're trying to move forward into a better future, for everyone."

"It's not what I need."

"What *do* you need?" Crystal said.

Before he could answer, she leaned in to Jordan and flicked her tongue across his earlobe.

"I need you to stop *that*," he said.

"No you don't," she said.

"Crystal . . ."

She seemed to swallow his ear hole. Her voice echoed in the caverns of his mind: "You don't want me to stop, you big, strong hero-man. You never want me to stop."

Jordan shuddered.

Crystal was licking his neck now. She had her hand on his thigh, kneading it in circles. Jordan felt his erection growing, against his will. This was another side effect of this program with Crystal. He always got hard, all the time, whether he wanted to or not, and soon enough, the lower demons took over and Crystal took full advantage.

Jordan just wanted to talk, to try and figure out where he stood—in relationship to her, to the MDC, to New Austin, and to the vast and mysterious universe that, thus far, was proving strangely disappointing. He had so many feelings to share. But Crystal never wanted to talk. She wanted to dominate. And dominate him she did.

With a touch of her index finger, Crystal deactivated Jordan's Dissolv-O Pants, which she forced him to wear. She pushed him back, slipped out of her robe, and mounted him, regally.

"Are you going to keep me safe, Jordan Kincaid?" she said as she rocked back and forth, "up there on that big scary mountain?"

"Y-yes," Jordan said. "I'll do anything for you."

"Just to be sure," she said, "you need to stay on your diet."

She slid a wafer in his mouth.

Jordan's doubts immediately began to dissolve. He was just strength and sensation now, one of two ideal humans fucking madly at the very pinnacle of a glistening empire. The city cast its sustainable phosphorescence over their ideal forms. This was what everyone wanted out of life.

Jordan flipped Crystal over on her back, placed his mouth on hers, and thrust into her, hard.

"Fuck me away, you perfect Earth animal!" she said.

Jordan did as commanded.

He was a good servant.

Tomorrow they would go to the mountain.

21

Olympus Mons sat two hundred and fifty miles away from the New Austin dome, due west, hugging the equator. Developers had initially wanted to put the city even closer, but the mountain's astonishing girth disrupted the planetary winds, strengthening them far beyond their normal speed, intermittently filling the air with ten-mile-wide clouds of dust. This wasn't the synthetic stuff that the kids liked to snort. It choked the sky in an endless red storm. No life could survive near the mountain for long.

Yet there it stood, tantalizingly close, a thing for humanity to conquer, or at least get near. Most Martian residents had neither the time nor the resources to escape the bubble, where chaos and low gravity reigned. If they did, it was usually because of some kind of dreadful work detail where the fatality rate hovered around 75 percent. The lucky ones got to be Sherpas for the vacation class. It was a lot of work, but it included tips, and the rich were paranoid about lawsuits, so they kept the mortality rates relatively low. If ten Sherpas left on a trip, eight came home on average.

Sonia had yoked Leonard to a cart like a space-ox. The cart rolled under its own power. He just had to operate the directional device. Still, he had to remain tied to the front in case of some sort of malfunction.

Fuck this shit, he thought.

Leonard liked the partying part of the revolution, but work had never been his thing. At least this job didn't require much concentration. He took a puff off his porto-vape, which he did approximately once every five minutes.

They hadn't told him what his cart contained; the contents remained secret to the Sherpas. Some of them carried food, some had perfumed flowers and bedsheets, others hauled important people in individual office pods, while others drew a bad lot and got tied to sloshing toilets. Only the unionized roadies, who hauled all musical instruments and gear, knew what was in their cargo. They weren't supposed to know, but they were badass. No one messed with them roadies or their tricked-out hover-cycles.

The line of Sherpas had moved slowly all day through the southeast end of town, to a tract of land that had once been a fecal dump and an enormous soybean farm. After the farm fell prey to an indigenous Martian bug that secreted sodium hydrochloride from its testicles, the MDC filled in and paved over the entire acreage, building in its place an enormous hermetically sealed hangar that started aboveground but gradually went beneath the Martian surface. The hangar housed an expensive outlet mall, several secret nightclubs and restaurants, and an emergency transmission station for Device podcasters who found themselves bothered by anarchist program hacks. It was a private place where people could go to just chill.

Sonia, who had wrangled her way into a supervisory role, walked up and down the line, making eye contact with her people, who were spaced throughout evenly, most of them secretly armed. She came up to Leonard.

"How are you handling it?" she said.

"I'm bored," he said. "I want some better weed."

"Can't you stay sober?" she said.

"No," said Leonard.

She had serious doubts about him, but he was one of the few people she knew who'd shown even a modicum of competence out in the Martian wild. There was no choice but to place him in an important spot.

"What am I carrying?" Leonard said.

"I can't tell you."

She had a master chart.

"Oh, come on!" Leonard said. "I have to cruise two hundred miles over the Martian surface for four days, and you're not going to tell me who or what or why?"

"Fine," she said, leaning in. She whispered, "You are carrying three passengers: Jonathan Bartholomew, the novelist who wrote *Beyond the Ever Forever*; his wife Carol Rothbart, who developed the storytelling software for Device 10; and Leora Achebe-Finkelstein-Chao, the head of the Interplanetary Anti-Hunger Initiative."

"Important people!" Leonard said.

"Eh, they're just another elite sex triad who use the Summit Summit as an excuse for outdoor fucking," Sonia corrected him.

The line of Sherpas stopped.

They had arrived at the gate.

Sonia walked up to the functionary who manned the controls and handed him a ream of paperwork. The functionary gave it a cursory look, and he pulled a lever.

The door of the hangar opened, twenty feet high and twenty feet wide, like the jaws of a great beast. Before him, Leonard beheld the whirling desolation of the Martian surface, a million miles of hell buffeted by relentless poison winds.

It was vacation time.

The great impermeable moving dome moved out of the larger dome. It was as though New Austin itself were giving birth to a nutrient-rich municipal amoeba. If cities reproduced, this is how they would do it: by disgorging their elite and their handpicked servants, contained within a shell that was five times more secure than the original shell.

Ideas blossomed. Style germinated. Science happened in a party atmosphere.

This was the Summit Summit.

The moving dome moved long and lean, a synthetic monster-worm. It rolled forward at a steady pace, and all the carts rolled with it. Leonard sat in his side chair, watching the blasted landscape pass by, fully aware that five unprotected seconds in that atmosphere would mean that he'd float away and vaporize. Inside the moving dome, though, gravity was 90 percent of Earth levels and the atmosphere was clean and vaguely redolent of fresh herbs. Sonia moved through the dome on her hover-pedi, looking very serious.

She flew by Leonard and hovered there, looking out at the land-scape with him.

"They would develop all this land if they could," she said.

"Fuck," Leonard said. "They can *have* it."

"Don't say that," she said. "People need a place to live."

People have a place to live now, he thought to himself. Yeah, it was a little overcrowded and pretty expensive, but the food was good and there was lots of partying. That's what Leonard had expected from Mars. Getting involved in a violent people's revolution, on the other hand, seemed like a lot of work. He was actively starting to think about bail-ing after this expedition, trying to find Jordan, maybe getting a job or something. If this stupid planet had a place for him, he hoped to Gaia it wasn't hauling around a rich novelist couple and their humanitarian fuck-toy.

He could feel their vibrations in his seat.

"If the hover-pod is rockin'," they had warned him in training, "don't come a knockin'."

His interest was low regardless.

Leonard handed Sonia his vape. Much to her surprise, she took a puff.

"I thought you didn't do drugs," he said.

"Dude," she said. "You thought wrong. I just don't do them all the time like you do. This week is stressful."

They cruised along in stoned silence. Dusk arrived. The air glowed orange, a warning of the icy night to come. In the distance, outside the dome, Leonard saw figures, shuffling. The dome grew closer, and the figures grew larger.

They stood at least ten feet tall, their faces and bodies mostly hidden beneath great cloaks, save some webbed, six-toed feet, which clung to the soil like roots. Three of them led a braying beast of burden that appeared to have eight layers of natural fur.

What is in this weed? he thought.

"*Who*," he said, "is *that*?"

"Didn't you know?" Sonia said. "Martians are real."

Leonard blinked at them. "Are you sure?"

"Pretty sure."

"How many of them are there?"

"No one knows," she said. "We know they exist because they occasionally come up to the edge of the dome and peer in. There's been a little dusty drone footage. They're pretty secretive."

"Wow, I'd sure like to meet them someday."

The Martians, for their part, regarded the moving dome nervously. These Earth things had constructed something modest, almost like an amusement park, a commendable achievement. But now they were starting to leave the nest. Martians had long life spans and a kind of genetic second sight that could allow them to predict two hundred years into the future with 60 percent accuracy. They'd been monitoring for centuries. They knew that when it came to humans, beware the westward wagon train.

But the average human had no interest in, or even awareness of ,indigenous Martians. They cared more about the cellular consistency of ramen noodles or the fat content of their bacon. Night had almost fallen, and that meant dinnertime. With a great whistle, the moving dome stopped.

Leonard sighed and unbuckled his safety belt. This was the part of the day where he actually had to work. He got down from his perch and walked over to the pod entrance, knocking three times, as per protocol.

"Yesssss?" he heard a voice say from inside.

"Cocktails are served on the chairman's veranda," he said, as he'd been told to say.

"Just a second!" said another voice.

Leonard idly puffed his vape. The pod door opened. Out stepped the novelist and the literary Device developer and the intergalactic humanitarian, looking flushed and ruffled.

"My," said the novelist, "what an invigorating conversation that was about intergalactic affairs!"

"We achieved a new synthesis of ideas," said his wife, the app developer. "My brain is simply blooming with new connections."

"I think I need to change my panties," said the humanitarian, and she rushed back inside the pod. Leonard offered the couple a puff of his vape.

"I have my own," said the man.

"We get ours through the Exchange," she said. "We don't have to smoke street weed."

Snobbery prevailed, here as in all places.

The pods had been drawn into a circle, with the personal pods at the inner level, the provisions next, and the back rows for the support materials and workingmen's toilets. The personal pods all came en suite, of course. In the center, workers were busy setting up a buffet tent, a liquor tent, and a party-drug tent. Leonard's job was to lay out the blankets for his people and to present them with a roll of drink tickets, limitless yet necessary as symbols of Dick Waters's legendary generosity to Mars's leading citizens. Picnics were in fashion.

It would be a picnic to end all picnics, with Dick Waters footing the bill. As the outermost wagons circled, the champagne flowed freely. It was another delightfully endless Martian twilight on the patio. The sky turned rose, save for a penumbra of sky blue around the setting sun. Wasn't it marvelous to dine alfresco? The Martian cultural elite would picnic their asses off all week long.

Weebly Crothers, the serialized holography editor for the *Martian Chronicle*, was in tight conversation with Kristoff Gloom, who had invented a Device function that allowed consumers to bank in reverse, making it seem like they were saving money when they were actually spending nearly twice as much. Chef Ellen Woo, the founder of Martian minimalist cooking, played chess with Christianne Aranciata, whose holistic lifestyle tips and news bulletins reached more than eighty million people daily on five planets and/or moons.

But mostly, it was writers and filmmakers who'd come to worship at the temple of this lord of money. They had no choice. Since all movies and books and holographic serials were now free to the public, artists had to cater to the rich in order to be fed and supported in their work. The MDC wrote the checks and gave out the awards. No wonder that esteemed novelist Jonathan Richard Bachmann's most recent three-volume work, *Development*, was little more than a largely favorable, moderately fictionalized history of the MDC.

Dick Waters appeared on the stage, his artificial skin mocha and wrinkle free, his teeth very polished, his long blond wig flowing in the artificial breeze. His daughter, Crystal, stood next to him, wearing what everyone else was wearing but making it look a hundred times better. On Waters's other side stood a stoic, frighteningly armored man whose face was obscured by a full-length smartvisor.

Behold the rulers of Mars.

"My friends," Dick Waters said, "it's been a long but productive year. The MDC's thirty-year plan for stability is nearly complete. And you all have been part of it. As you know, I like to bring all the important people together to talk, and to think, and to remember how far we've come. This is where ideas happen; this is where lifelong friends are made, where coalitions form. This is where serialized holographic animated GIF series get pitched to over-the-top entertainment service providers."

The audience laughed, but it was true. Without the Summit Summit, there would be no holographic Mangapus. That deal had been cut a few years ago at the base of Olympus Mons's fabulous red nipple, and many people had gotten richer as a result.

"But most of all," Dick Waters said, his teeth flashing, his arms held wide as if to embrace this very small, extraordinarily fortunate percentage of the world, "this is where we party! Let the Summit Summit begin!"

He raised his arms over his head.

Nothing happened.

"Where's the music?" Dick Waters shouted. "Where is the motherfucking light show? Goddamn mothertossing incompetent shitball rat-eating Gaia-raping bitch-holing yoga-doing fuck fuck fucking fuckers! Why do I never get what I want?"

"Calm down, Daddy," said Crystal Waters.

She motioned to the bodyguard to take the old nut away. Without a blink, she turned to the crowd and said, "Sorry, guys, you know what Dad is like. He needs a little warm toddy and a nap. Travel can be hard on a grumpy old coot."

The crowd, which had been shuffling uncomfortably, relaxed and laughed. They loved Crystal. Her dad had the empire, for now. But she was the future and set the tone for the present.

"So I'm just gonna go back to his pod and make sure that he gets tucked in nice and that his fake skin doesn't get wrinkled when they hang it up, and then I'm going to personally inject him with sleep drugs. And I'll see you all later. In the meantime, enjoy your picnic."

There was a distinct sense of relief among the gathered. Their postures relaxed; they began to lounge in earnest. Crystal waved her hand. The music started and so did the light show. Out of nowhere, fashionable waitstaff appeared, bearing trays of Venusian rum cocktails and Nevada wines, and platters of the finest marijuana in the Milky Way, grown on a Mercury-orbiting hothouse satellite. The cultural elite began to spark up. Some of them danced. In far corners of the traveling dome, the Mars Dust was coming out as well.

Sonia Smartphone scooted about in her supervisory role. She had all the Sherpas on her team, the members of the waitstaff who weren't trying to parlay this gig into an acting role, some of the personal attendants, all of the cooks, various other serfs, and, most importantly, the sanitary engineers. They who control the shit control the battle.

She surveyed the dome as best she could, memorizing all the entrances and exits, probing for weak points in the structure where they could plant bombs. Security seemed fairly light, actually. Dick Waters always had elite soldiers, but there only seemed to be about a dozen of them spaced out at decent intervals, and maybe another three or four who were roaming around the crowd, at a respectful distance. They appeared to have enough firepower to provide basic security, but not much more.

Sonia hovered, nodding at her people, all of them very well briefed and ready to go to the wall for her. These were the working people, the real people of Mars. Sonia had to fight for them: the displaced, the children of the displaced, the soon-to-be displaced, the culturally marginal. Didn't the city belong to them, too? Wasn't their voice worth something?

Sonia couldn't believe what Mars had become. This was why her grandfather had worked so hard and her father had slacked so efficiently? So a bunch of preening trendoid assholes could do their drugs and write their serialized cartoon novellas sixteen stories above everyone else? So you could wait five hours in line for a basket of mediocre fried chicken with cheddar hushpuppies?

It would all change soon.

Sonia pulled up next to Leonard, who was puffing on a joint the size of a sausage while also drinking a very large mug of beer.

"What's up, Captain Smartphone?" he said.

"Everyone is ready," she said.

"Right on!"

"Tomorrow, we march to the base of Olympus Mons. There, Mars will meet its destiny."

"Cool!" Leonard said, handing her the joint. "You want some?"

"Gaia yes," said Sonia. "I am so stressed out."

She dismounted and took a drag big enough to stun a horse, exhaling all the pressures of the day.

"Things have to change, Leonard," she said. "They have to."

"They're gonna change no matter what," he said.

"Yeah, but—oh, you don't understand."

"Nope," Leonard said, taking a huge drag. "I sure don't."

"Damn it," said Sonia. "I really hope this plan works."

22

From the New Austin dome, Olympus Mons barely registered, a wide, dark tumor in the neon-tinted dust. Unlike volcanoes on Earth, which are forever being pushed upward by the rotation of the planetary crust, Olympus Mons spread high and wide. Mars's crust is stationary, and the lava flows in streams.

From above, Olympus Mons appears completely massive, but it spreads wide, in distinct layers, making the summit look less like a peak and more like a massive galactic aureole. This view had inspired generations of schoolchildren to great hilarity. "I saw your mom's Olympus Mons" became a grievous schoolyard insult. It was the biggest breast in the solar system.

They traveled all the next day. As they drew closer to the great mountain, it actually seemed to disappear in front of them. Width replaced height but also combined with it. The cliffs of Olympus Mons stretch thousands of feet high, dozens of Everests woven together, casting shadows for hundreds of miles. By afternoon, the shadows had grown so deep and cold that they had to turn on the lights in the great moving dome and turn the heat close to max. The atmosphere inside the dome grew tense and fearful.

Crystal Waters, who had been through this every year since the beginning, felt unfazed by fear or doubt or anything else. The MDC first inspired awe in people, then showed them how that awe could be conquered, and that pretty much silenced all but the most outlier critics. This Summit Summit dance served as a reward to those who'd played the game most effectively. And when they got to the base of the cliffs of Olympus Mons, everyone would see exactly what the MDC could do.

"How are we going to get *up* that thing?" people were saying, not unreasonably, as the mountain edge neared. Even if they had been in good physical condition—which they certainly were not—they didn't have hiking equipment, not that any hiking equipment ever created was going to be able to get more than a hundred people, plus their servants, up the sheerest cliff in the known galaxy, on a planet with 10 percent gravity and an unbreathable atmosphere.

"What are we going to do now?"

This doubt, this almost-fear, was exactly what the MDC wanted.

The caravan stopped. Crystal Waters appeared on the dome-screen, wearing a fetchingly adventurous outfit.

"Well, we've made it this far," she said.

Nervous laughter moved throughout the line.

"Now, the one thing we always say at Summit Summit is: you can talk about anything that goes on here, as long as you don't leak any documents about how much it cost."

More laughter.

"But the one thing you absolutely must keep quiet, the secret that is totally inviolable is"—Crystal paused for effect—"how to get up the mountain."

There were a number of reasons why the MDC didn't want the general population to know how it had scaled the cliffs of Olympus Mons. One, they were still seeking to secure certain galactic patents for their methods, which they rushed into without testing out bugs. The last thing they needed was meddling from Earth bureaucrats. Two, they wanted knowledge to leak out about it gradually, so as to control the flow of tourists from other planets. Three, if the people of Mars ever found out how much money and resources they'd actually spent on the project, they'd burn down MDC headquarters in a people's revolution that would make the Great Bronx Uprising of 2115 seem like a skirmish by comparison. It had been expensive.

"For the last fifteen years," Crystal went on, "the MDC has been working on a way to ascend Olympus Mons safely and with minimal effort. We believe this land has the potential to be a vacation paradise where all the best minds of Mars can come to relax, renew, restore, and revisit what's truly important. Now, we're still at the early phases of development, which is why we've essentially installed you in a portable hotel suite, but with contributions from Mars's leading citizens, we can turn the Summit Summit into a six- or seven-month-a-year occurrence, with both cabanas for rent and time-shares. Just something to think about. In any case, tonight, we're going to camp. There's not a surprise spa for you up at the top."

There was more general laughter. Crystal could say anything to this crowd.

"What we have done, though," she said, "is construct a *way* to the top. Lights!"

With that, the dome went dark, and great floodlights shone upon the cliff. A section had been carved out. It was smooth and sloped upward, gently, through the human-created canyon.

"This ramp is gravitationally magnetized," she said. "It is attuned to the energy vibrations of our moving dome. Nothing else has to move at all. The dome just floats on up."

There were general *oohs* and *aahs* from the crowd.

Sonia wasn't as pleased. She hadn't factored this into the plan. On night two, the Summit Summit guidebook said they camped at the base of Olympus Mons, near here. But there had been no mention of this magnetized-ramp thing. That secret had definitely held.

And now what? She had bombs planted to go off throughout the dome. There was no way to dial back the timer. And she didn't have any reliable way to communicate back to the city, not from all the way out here. She had to manage a team of several dozen people, and now she was going to have to completely pivot.

"Leonard," she whispered.

"What?"

"You need to get the word out. We need to be ready. At any moment."

"Ready for what?"

"For anything."

Whatever the anarchists were going to try, the elevator was ready to ride. More than 1,700 moon-slaves had died constructing it, at a cost of 576 trillion credits. Crystal planned to use it.

"Let's head on up!" she said.

The dome inched forward, and then it caught. The whole structure hitched once, like it was going over an especially large speed bump. That was going to have to be smoothed out. But then it began to glide, ever so slowly, up the greatest mountain on Mars.

◆ ◆ ◆

They crawled up all night, ten relaxing miles of endless picnics and conversation and classic twenty-third-century lounge music. While the guests kicked back, sipping lemon-ginger soda laced with indica oil that would help them fall asleep, the staff worked triple-time to keep them relaxed, which in turn stressed the staff, which made their work even harder. Sonia didn't have time to visit—much less remember—all of her team, to try to brief them on a plan that she hadn't even entirely rewritten yet. What if she told someone who wasn't in on it, and that person told Crystal Waters? They'd all be executed on the spot.

Leonard remained surprisingly chill. "It will all work out fine," he said. "Everything always does."

"We've got them outnumbered," Sonia said, "but we're volunteers, most of whom haven't executed more than a pipe bomb in a tapas bar. This has got to move perfectly."

"Steady under pressure, boss," Leonard said.

They reached the top of the cliffs just as the novelists were waking up to a gourmet breakfast. The elevator deposited them into a metal tunnel. When the last inch was safely on rock, the dome began to move forward under its own stored power, through the tunnel and onto the surface. Sonia took a quick survey. There were rock outcroppings. This was good. If the battle got forced onto the surface, they could fight guerilla-style.

On the other hand, the surface seemed to be pocked by little bloops of lava. This mountain didn't erupt. It oozed constantly, like untended interstellar acne. The dome had to put on its heat-protection layer, the kind of technology that only top-enders could afford. Even in the spacesuit that everyone, employee or guest, had been issued, it would be hard to stand on that surface for more than fifteen minutes without overheating, or, worse, getting swallowed by a surprise burp of Martian lava.

Before, they were just going to seize control of the dome, turn it around, and march back to New Austin triumphant. Now they found themselves stuck here on this *thing*, with the means of exit sealed shut behind them. No one in her cohort knew how to operate a giant gravity elevator. She just had to hope they didn't kill the person who did.

These were the crème de Mars. Never again would so many prominent people be so helpless in the same place at the same time. The minutes ticked away on their golden brunch hour. Sonia started nodding to those who were near her. Leonard moved to her right flank, and someone equally brave and foolish to her left.

The wagons had circled.

Sonia hovered on her pedi.

Crystal Waters took the stage.

"Well, here we are," she said. "Isn't it spectacular? The thermal activity, I hear, is good for your pores."

The elite laughed, transfixed by her words as usual.

"I have to apologize," she said. "My father isn't going to join us again tonight. The atmosphere is a little thin up here, and the old baboon needs his oxygen. But that's OK. We have more fun without him. Kidding, Dad!" She leaned in to the audience. "Not kidding," she whispered.

Yet another aspect of Sonia's plan had fallen apart. She'd intended to get Dick Waters to confess to his crimes against the Martian people. If he refused, she'd kill him. Either way, she'd take the dome home and proclaim a new democratic Mars.

But suddenly she realized she was leading a group of untrained, drug-addled rock 'n' roll morons into a battle they couldn't possibly win. They were encased in technology they didn't know how to operate, separated by inches from a smoldering lava pit they couldn't control. But Sonia had no choice. The bombs were set. She sent out the signal.

Sonia accelerated the pedi, hovered for a second above the platform where Crystal Waters stood, and then flipped a somersault off the bike, landing behind Crystal and grabbing her. The bike hovered down after her. Her lieutenants flanked her on either side, holding shotguns that they'd stowed away in their housing units. About the dome, other rebels sprung up, aiming straight at security guards and at key installation and engineering points.

"On behalf of the Martian resistance!" Sonia said bravely. "I claim control of this expedition!"

The music stopped.

"What?" someone said from the crowd.

"I said the resistance has seized control!"

"Is this part of the program?" someone else said.

"No, damn it, no! This is open rebellion!"

"Fuck you!" someone shouted.

"Where are our appetizers?" shouted someone else.

Sonia nodded her head. A gunshot sounded. The person who'd asked for appetizers fell dead. He was only MDC's Vice Minister in Charge of Device Advertising for Exterior Planets and had been schedule to retire anyway, but people screamed anyway when his body crumpled to the floor of the dome.

"Quiet!" Sonia shouted. "Anyone else have comments for me?"

"I've got one," Crystal Waters said.

"You get to talk *enough*," Sonia said. "We're taking you out. We're taking out the whole machine."

"Oh, are you?" said Crystal. "What do you think got you to the top of this mountain? What do you think built this dome? Or New Austin, for that matter? The *machine* that you hate so much is the only reason you're here at all."

"That's a lie," said Sonia. She shouted to the crowd: "I was here *before* the MDC! They didn't build Mars. My family did, and families like my family. We built it with our hands and our hearts. Mars isn't about the MDC. Mars belongs to the people!"

The revolutionaries gave a shout, the dome reverberating with the first possibility of actual revolution. Even a few expeditioneers applauded lightly. That got shut down fast by nasty glances from their triad partners.

"That's a very noble sentiment," Crystal said. "And it's true that some families get displaced in the development process—"

"Displaced!" Sonia said. "You all *murdered* my father, you bitch!"

"Let me finish," Crystal said. "Do you really think people on Mars want a revolution? To go back to a time where children were getting kidnapped in the streets and sold to moon slavers? When the city's main amphitheater was used as a shelter for hop junkies? Where the garbage union went on strike for a month and twenty thousand people died from spore poisoning? That stuff doesn't happen when we're in charge."

"You don't own this planet!" Sonia said. "No one does!"

"I have documents that argue otherwise."

"Fuck your documents!" Sonia said. "Your day is done. When the resistance takes control, Mars will automatically become affordable for middle-class families again!"

"We're building a thousand units a month—"

"No more lies!" Sonia said. "You're going to die now."

While the revolutionaries cocked their guns, Crystal nodded upward. Above in the shadows, Jordan Kincaid crouched on a beam, aiming his pea gun of death right at Sonia Smartphone's jugular vein. He fired.

Sonia dropped to her knees, clutching her neck, a look of shock in her eyes, a gusher of blood pushing against her hand. With her other hand, she reached for Leonard.

"Bike," she croaked.

Chaos erupted in the dome. The artsy set bolted for their trailers. Crystal ducked away, flecks of blood on her shoulders, to her private quarters. Her father sat in a warm sitz bath, barely registering sound.

"Is everything OK?" he said. "I heard a noise."

"Everything is fine," she said. "It's as we predicted. Jordan and his people are taking them out."

"Fucking anarchists," said Waters. "Captain Ted and his ideas can rot in hell."

Most anarchists had dropped their guns and fled immediately, hoping to blend back in. A few fired back at the MDC forces. They got shot down quickly.

A small group had managed to circle a few trailers. They were crouched in the middle of them and shooting out. Jordan Kincaid jumped from the ceiling into the center of the circle. He whirled his leg around in a circle, knocking heads. These bastards meant nothing to him.

Leonard had dragged Sonia off the stage, the blood gushing from her neck. He had his protective suit on, but it wasn't protecting him from getting splattered.

"The bombs," she said. "Get . . ."

"Get what?"

"The detonator, in my pack."

Leonard reached into Sonia's side pack. There was a small detonating device.

"Press it," she said. "Disrupt everything."

Leonard did. No bombs exploded. The detonator made a little fizzing sound.

"Shit," Sonia said.

The resistance never had the budget for decent technology.

"You have to get the hover-pedi back to New Austin," she said, "to let them know what happened."

"I can't do that. It's two hundred miles and down a mountain. In Martian winds."

"If anyone can, it's you, Leonard."

"What?"

"You're very calm."

"That's true," Leonard said. "Now come on, I'll take you with me. There's room for two."

"I'm not going anywhere," she said. "I made a mistake. We should have just waited this one out."

"Come on . . ."

"I tried," Sonia said. "It's your revolution now."

And then she died, her broken, defeated face in Leonard Tolliver's lap.

"Fuck," Leonard said.

There was no time for sentimentality, not even time to take much-needed drugs. Leonard hopped on the hover-pedi, pulled a fully pressurized helmet out of the rear compartment, put it on, set the oxygen supply for five hours and the gravity control to 12, and whooshed toward the emergency exit. The disturbance had been put down. He was the only one left.

At the exit stood a guard, the toughest-looking one of all. With his visor down, he looked like a whole army unto himself. Why the guard didn't vaporize him right there, Leonard didn't know. Maybe he was the one MDC employee with a soul.

"You going somewhere, freedom fighter?" he said.

"Come on, man, give me a break," Leonard said. "I didn't ask for this shit. I just came to Mars to party. Let me out of here on the ten-percent chance I make it back to New Austin alive."

The solider looked at Leonard as though he were some sort of artifact. He pressed the button. The emergency tube opened. The soldier moved off to the side. Leonard paused and hovered.

"Get out of here before I shoot off your head," said the soldier.

"Roger that," Leonard said. He whooshed out the door, up into the sky, over the rim of the largest volcano in the solar system, and down to the Martian surface toward the lights of the only available city.

The guard closed the hatch. He lifted up his visor. It was Jordan.

"Leonard, you're an idiot," he said.

23

The time had come for the Mars by Mars festival, but really, it was always time. More or less the entire Martian year was spent either planning MBM or cleaning up and recovering from MBM. The festival lasted three months, and it sometimes took people three additional months to get from Earth and then three months to get back. This meant that support staff for the next year's MBM began to arrive before the previous year's cleanup crew left. Lots of people never left, though, not because Mars was so much better than Earth—it wasn't—but because MBM had either chewed up all their money or there was really no other way for them to make a living. Celebrating Mars was a full-time job for countless thousands.

It hadn't always been so. The Mars by Mars festival (or "Mars By," as Earth tourists liked to call it) started decades before the MDC ever set up shop. A mixed-gender banjo picker named Roscoe Anne McGonigle had the idea to stage a daylong concert on her twelve-acre property on the outskirts of what was then a much smaller New Austin. She set up a makeshift adobe stage, as wood was in short supply, ordered thirty genetically modified 3-D turkeys from a local manufacturer, dug a deep roasting pit, and invited all her friends in bands to come by and sit a spell and play some good old down-home Martian folk music. It went on for three whole days, as everyone celebrated that frontier spirit that made New Austin, and Mars itself, such a special place. They took pride in being known as "The Forgotten Planet" and "Earth's Worst Investment."

The next ten years went, more or less, the same as the first. Maybe a couple hundred additional locals heard about Roscoe Anne's Turkey Roast, but it still stayed very down-home, very real. Then came the food-shortage years and the mine collapse, and people started bailing on downtown, headed back to Earth, where they could have Enough. But Roscoe Anne held on stubbornly to her land and kept bringing people in every year. She sold off an acre to a quicklime consortium, putting the proceeds into her "turkey fund."

On the twelfth year of the Turkey Roast, the dust swirled red and thick on the surface for months, making the New Austin dome feel heavy, like a citywide prison. Little fissures began to open on the edges. Crews worked day and night to keep the atmosphere from collapsing, but then they went on strike. The atmosphere *did* collapse in part of Southeast New Austin, space-sucking away the souls of countless thousands. That was the final blow. All the industry left downtown, fleeing for greener Venusian lands or for the Central Antarctic Development Zone. Downtown was a rotting hulk, left for junkies and criminals. The artists and musicians stayed on the outskirts because it was cheap and because they had nowhere else to go.

Roscoe Anne held the Turkey Roast anyway. The people came in rags, flying the tattered red-and-gold Martian flag. They were alone in the universe. No corporation or government could save them. They had nothing. Roscoe Anne McGonigle cranked up the generator so they could hear some music.

At twilight on the third day, she took the stage herself, a lone man-woman-man-then-woman again. She wore a Martian flag bandana and a simple peasant jumpsuit and boots.

"Y'all been through it," she said, strumming her banjo, "like me. But we've done it together. We're Martians, and that's what Martians do. We ain't gonna let no food and energy shortage or a fatal oxygen leak bring us down. We know this land. We work this land. We're from this land. And we're gonna stay here, together."

Roscoe Anne McGonigle took a big drag from a fat blunt of Martian homegrown ditch dust, and began to sing:

We'll get along
Without our cars.
Mars by Mars.
Our Devices may
Run out of bars.
Mars by Mars.
They say that jobs are scarce,
And the air's not safe to breathe,
But when you grow up Martian,
You wear that on your sleeve.
We'll live without an atmosphere.
We'll wait for rockets to appear.
We'll only drink recycled beer.
Mars by Mars.

A hush moved over the crowd as they aimed their Devices toward the stage, recording this precious moment in galactic time. This was the song of the moment, and this was the moment for all hillbilly transgender space pioneers to stand up and be counted.

We'll keep our food
In storage jars.
Mars by Mars.
We'll proudly show

Our battle scars.
Mars by Mars.
They say the planet's done
And that it's time to leave,
But when you grow up Martian,
There are things you don't achieve.
We'll live each day like we don't care.
We'll pick dust mites out of our hair.
We'll only breathe recycled air.
Mars by Mars.

She paused, took a deep breath, and then sang, with tears in her eyes:

BYE-BYE, MARS.

By then, everyone was a blubbering mess, full of nostalgia for the days when the planet had made it work, a golden era of space. Footage of the song circulated around Mars that day, and people filled with genuine Martian pride. The theme made it onto the Devices of people who were taking the next rocket out, trying to leave as fast as possible because they never knew when the fuel was going to disappear, and within months, everyone on Earth was singing "Mars by Mars," too, and everyone knew about the Turkey Roast.

The next year, the Martian Development Corporation showed up.

One day, two ambitious young Earthmen rode their rented three-pronged dirt hoverers out beyond the limits of the mapped city. The air around Roscoe Anne's property was flat and cool, the soil untilled. Her simple three-room Martian mud house sat at the center of a landscape dotted with scrub and cacti that had been imported from Arizona centuries before. All those years, it had mostly fended for itself, as Martian-adaptable species did.

Roscoe Anne answered the door after a spell. She'd been sampling pickles in the cellar. Most of the time, she didn't get visitors, save for Turkey Roast time. She opened it to find two young men staring at her. They had clean jumpers on, which meant they weren't Martian.

"Help you?" she said.

One of the men, teeth gleaming artificially, said, "Ms. McGonigle?"

"Yes?"

He extended a hand. "Dick Waters," he said.

"OK."

"I'm the chairman of the Martian Development Corporation."

"Never heard of it."

"We're new in town. This is my associate, Ruben Kincaid."

The other man shook her hand as well. "A lovely piece of property you have here, ma'am," he said.

"It's mine," she said. "I have the deed."

"Of course you do," said Dick Waters. "And we wouldn't dream of taking it away from you."

"We were deeply moved, ma'am, by your 'Mars by Mars' song," said the other one, who seemed to have more of a way with people. "A lot of people were. We've come a long way to talk to you about making it a more permanent part of Martian life. We think with your help, we can save this planet."

Roscoe Anne McGonigle looked the men up and down. She didn't have much judgment. This time of day, she was pretty zonked out on Mars Dust and kava cookies.

"Come on in, boys," she said. "I'll make you some tea."

And with that, Mars changed forever.

24

Leonard Tolliver pulled his hover-pedi up to the Black Pig long after midnight, not like the hour of the day mattered at the Pig. It only closed one hour a day for "cleaning," which actually meant "extra drinking." The Black Pig was always there.

It had been a hard day of carting around Earth dwellers. They'd been arriving by the hundreds, getting ready for Mars by Mars. There were support staff and tech specialists and equipment managers and logistical suppliers and brand marketers and sound engineers and corporate flunkies and random rich jerks and the woman who thought up the slogan "Mars by Mars: The Future of Now Is Tomorrow," as well as her six volunteer interns. Some people were independent, a calculated risk at Mars By. Sure, you could make more as a budtender on Mars in three months than you could in three years doing *anything* on Earth, but the prices were so inflated that you could easily find yourself ten times in a debt hole and trapped in space forever. This is why Leonard had stuck with the rebellion: it was cheap living. Also, he'd made a promise to its field general as she'd died.

But really, it was a cost factor.

Leonard sauntered in, wearing leather and denim, like a man who hadn't paid for his weed or whiskey in months. Sure enough, there was a shot and a joint waiting for him on the bar.

"*Mon general*," said the budtender.

"Howdy, cowboy," said Leonard. He slammed the shot and put the joint in his mouth. The budtender lit it. Leonard took a puff. The stress of the night evaporated quickly.

"What's going on around here?" Leonard said.

"Captain Ted is pontificating," said the budtender.

"What else is new?"

"You haven't been here for a Mars By," the budtender said. "He gets overexcited. Drinks too much coffee. Too much everything. Starts hatching plans. People start dying."

"They're dying already."

"Right," said the budtender. "But they *really* die during Mars By."

Leonard went upstairs. Twenty eager young recruits sat around the room on pillows, listening to Captain Ted, who looked as grizzled as old boot fabric, talk about the old days, when Mars was young. They sat rapt. He smoked a joint.

So we sat around that table, and the old lady made us tea. It tasted like dirt. It was dirt tea. People were poor then. They are poor now, too, but the MDC throws up distractions to make them think they're not. Anyway, she was really poor.

We said to her, "Well, Roscoe Anne, your 'Mars by Mars' song really touched a chord on Earth. It made people remember Mars, what had been so special about it in the first place. We realized what a unique culture you've got here. And we want to spread the word."

She seemed skeptical, but we'd worked it all out.

"We think the Turkey Roast is a special event, and we'd like to put it at the center of a festival."

"A festival?" she said.

"Yeah, we're thinking about naming it after your song. The Mars by Mars festival."

"OK," she said.

"It would be a celebration of all the art and culture on Mars."

"There ain't much art and culture," she said. "Folks is poor."

"You see," Dick said, "that's where we come in. There's tons of culture on Earth. Too much of it, really. We want to bring it here, to use it to help lift Mars up. We want Mars to be a culture planet."

"I don't get it."

"The theory is that we bring in people with certain abilities, some of them artistic, and we use that to transform the economy while providing them with modestly priced housing," said Ruben

"We'll let the market decide housing costs," Dick said. "But we definitely want to use the arts to transform Mars."

"So, you want to buy my Turkey Roast?" said Roscoe Anne.

"No, it would be the centerpiece! Of the entire New Austin economy!"

"People aren't going to work no more or nothin'?"

"No, they're going to work more. Culture is going to change things. You'll see."

"All right," she said. "I guess. It's just a Turkey Roast with some singin' at it."

"Exactly. That's Mars."

"OK, fine," she said. "Have that festival."

Captain Ted gave a little strum of the guitar that he didn't actually know how to play.

What she didn't know was that we'd already decided to have the festival. It was already on the way. There were two rocket ships full of painters and musicians and transgendered performance artists—you know, the kinds of people who make places worthwhile. We even thought of a slogan. "Keep Mars Weird." That stuck around a little, huh?

Ted's acolytes, most of whom had never known a Mars that wasn't "weird," nodded knowingly. They understood that weirdness was a lie propagated by a sinister real-estate industry. Back in the day, though, it had been a badge of honor.

They all came in and they sprayed up the buildings and were putting on these live sex shows and the music was superloud, but no one cared because no one lived there and all the crazy people and murderers were fuckin' in the streets. Meanwhile, out in the boonies, we had all these stages set up and the locals were doing their Martian dances and picking their banjos. There were fifteen hundred people at the Turkey Roast that year, and everyone got two turkeys. Things were going so well that Mars by Mars went on a week longer than it was supposed to. I thought it was fucking amazing, but Dick was not into it.

"These people are disgusting," he said. "What they do, what they say, what they look like."

"This is the future, man!" I said. "The frontier. Embrace it!"

The next two years, Mars by Mars just rocked. It was fuckin' great, man. Art was art, and no one messed with us. I was just like yeah, man, this is how it should be. Word got back to Earth, and the tourists started showing up. Just a few at first. People were streaming shit back to Earth, which hadn't seen a party like this in a long time, with all their boring concerts in the park.

Dick Waters was like, hey, man, we should take the Art Pad condo. That was this mammoth structure that used to be a dried-corn-powder warehouse until the dust mites got into it and the people bailed. People would hang out in there for days, just spray-painting each other and playing bumper-scooter and drinking beer and just fuckin', you know. And I said, come on, Dick, the Art Pad is for the people. He was like, the people are coming, *dude, and they're coming soon. We have to be ready. There need to be hotels and restaurants. They're going to want to buy investment condos.*

"Well," I say, "fuck investment condos." Right?

The kids all cheered. Leonard just watched Captain Ted do his shtick.

One day I came down and the Art Pad had a sign hanging out in front, "Future Home of Art Pad Lofts." The door was locked, and people were hanging out in front.

"All my supplies are in there, man," said an artist I knew.

"I'll take care of it," I said.

But when I found Dick Waters on the other side of the building, some unemployed guys—everyone was unemployed—were loading all the art supplies into a big incinerator-hauler.

"Hey, man," I said. "Don't fuck with art."

"Don't go native on me," Dick said. "This isn't art. It's garbage."

"People live here," I said. "This is where they create."

"They live here illegally," Dick said. "I got the government to pass a writ of eminent domain. The MDC owns the Art Pad now."

Captain Ted paused, took a drag, and sighed.

Six months later, when it was time again for Mars By, the lofts were open. Dick had started advertising Mars By to fraternal advertising societies. Those people will go to anything if you put the word drinks *on the flier. They were coming to Mars and snapping up property like candy. They'd come in on the Mars By rockets, and they'd just stay and keep on partying. On Earth, they had Enough, but on Mars, they lived like royalty. It was kind of unbelievable. Nothing changed on Mars for decades—well, nothing for the good—and then all of the sudden these huge buildings just started sprouting out of nowhere and all these people were hanging around wearing trendy clothes and just getting wasted all the time.*

Now, don't get me wrong, this made me really rich. I designed some kick-ass buildings. But I was getting worried. I said to Dick, "Aren't you worried that all this unchecked development is going to change what people liked about New Austin in the first place?" He laughed in my face. Straight up laughed, the prick. And he said, "Who cares? Keep Mars Weird, dude. Keep Mars Weird." That's when I knew we were really in trouble.

The city just kept growing beyond its original boundaries. The rockets kept landing, full of building materials, and people, and chemicals for making high-grade synthetic Mars Dust. After a decade, Mars by Mars was three months long, and by the end of it, every year, the city was twenty percent more crowded and twenty percent more expensive. It was bulging. It needed to grow.

By that time, people had forgotten about the Turkey Roast. Some of the originals still hauled out to Roscoe Anne's property. But the crowds weren't getting any larger. All the Mars by Mars marketing efforts were focused downtown, where all the loft buildings had performance stages and restaurants and holographic immersion theaters. Everyone wanted to hear the coolest bands play at the MDC tent complex, not go listen to some old tranny play the banjo on the dirt prairie.

"No one's going to give a shit if we take that bag's property away," Dick said to me.

"She might give a shit," I said.

"Let's see where we're at during Hangover Week," he said.

After Mars By, everyone slept for four days straight and then spent three days eating Vita-Ramen to recover. Just like now. Everyone except Dick Waters, who doesn't party. He only develops.

He woke me up at the Gaia-forsaken hour of noon thirty and told me to get dressed. We were going out to Roscoe Anne's property. Us and fifteen hover-cops and two vapo-tanks.

"What are those for?" I asked.

"Security," he said.

I could see why he wanted the land. New neighborhoods were pressing up against Roscoe Anne's property. We hovered through areas that had been bombed-out craters but now were full of families pushing hover-strollers and hot chicks in see-through yoga pants just busting out into headstands. But I didn't see why he needed security.

Roscoe Anne's land was trashed. There were turkey carcasses and beer-foam canisters and even a few people still crashed out in tents. I fucking loved it. This was Mars, and Mars had to be free.

"Anarchy," Dick said.

He hovered right up to Roscoe Anne's front porch, flanked by the beefiest security I'd ever seen, and knocked on her door.

It was a couple of long minutes before she appeared, looking older and more bedraggled than ever.

"Help you?" she said.

"I'm from the Martian Development Corporation, Ms. McGonigle. Maybe you remember me."

"I don't remember nothin'," she said.

"Well, I came here a number of years ago from Mars by Mars—"

"Mars by Mars is bullshit," she said. "It ain't done nothin' for me 'cept give me grief and people pukin' on my property."

"Funny you should say that. We want to alleviate your burden."

"What my what now?"

"We want to buy your land."

"I ain't sellin'."

"Now, be reasonable, Roscoe Anne," Dick said. "You're not getting any younger, and it's a lot of work to keep up your property and your house, and you can't get rid of the Turkey Roast."

"I get by fine," she said.

"No doubt, no doubt," said Dick. "But we are prepared to make you a very generous offer of two hundred sixty-five million credits—"

"I bought this land for seven hundred credits," she said.

"I know, that's what the deed says, so you would be making almost forty thousand times profit."

"Yeah, and I know how much it's worth. More like seven billion credits."

"We're prepared to give you up to four hundred million," Dick said. "Right now. On the spot. Today."

"Where would I go?"

"We'd give you two, maybe three months to get your affairs in order. Then the development process—"

"No sale," she said, and she slammed the door.

Dick stood on the deck, fuming. "That senile old bag can't turn us down," he said.

"What did you expect?" I said. "We'll just build around her. She'll die soon enough, and then maybe we can place her land into some kind of public trust, like a Mars by Mars park—"

"I had enough public trusts on Earth. That's why I came to Mars, so I could actually own some land. A man has to make money somewhere in the galaxy."

"But you do make money," I said. "Tons of money."

"Not Enough!" he said.

"When is it going to be Enough?"

"I'll let you know."

He knocked on Roscoe Anne's door again. She answered after a while.

"I said no," she said.

"We're prepared to offer you five hundred million credits for your land," he said.

"No."

"Six hundred million."

"I ain't sellin'."

"OK, we'll give you seven hundred fifty million," he said. "But we cannot possibly go any higher."

Roscoe Anne stood there for a second, pondering. "Just a second," she said.

She went back inside. Dick gave me a knowing smirk. I wasn't so sure.

Roscoe Anne's door opened. She stood there pointing a shotgun at our heads.

"Now git off my property, or I will blow off your face," she said. "I've done it before to poachers. And you're the biggest poacher I ever met."

"I'm sure we can be reasonable," Dick said.

"You ain't gonna be reasonable," she said. "I know you. I've been following you on the holo-news. You come to Mars and you talk all this talk

and you put up all these buildings. But it don't mean shit. Mars is bigger than you are."

"Now—"

Roscoe Anne cocked the hammer. "Git!" she exclaimed.

Dick Waters raised a finger.

From a distance, the vapo-cannon fired.

Roscoe Anne disintegrated into a pile of dust.

"It's our land now," Dick Waters said.

Captain Ted paused, mournfully. This story still affected him, after all these years. He took a big swallow of Martian still moonshine.

"I was so angry, I didn't know what to do," Captain Ted said. "This wasn't why we'd come to Mars, to kill old ladies and take their land. I wanted to strangle Dick right there. But I couldn't. There was security. He always had the best. So instead I spat in his face. He looked surprised.

"Mars by Mars can go fuck itself," I said.

"I got on my hoverer and came right here to the Black Pig and got drunker than I'd ever been before. By the end of the night I'd torn off my MDC clothes and some chick from Luna was tattooing 'Fuck the MDC' on my chest. I shattered my fucking Device and went underground. That was the night that Captain Ted was born. That was the night I pledged to destroy the MDC. That was the night that Ruben Kincaid ceased to exist."

Leonard spit out his drink.

"You got a problem, Tolliver?" said Captain Ted. "I'm trying to motivate the troops here."

"Did you say Ruben Kincaid?" Leonard said.

"That was my name," Captain Ted said. "Don't wear it out."

This is bad, Leonard thought.

Did Jordan know?

25

Jordan Kincaid, who did not know, walked the streets of New Austin, heavily armed and hiding in the shadows. The deterrent police cruised around low on hover-pedis or installed themselves in booths in the rowdiest clubs and restaurants (the public sections only; VIPs were never policed); that kept things mostly under control. But Jordan didn't fall into their category. His entire existence was off the books, all evidence of him erased from the databases. He didn't draw a pension. It was possible that he didn't even draw a salary. He didn't know. Crystal took care of all his needs, material and otherwise. He wasn't a deterrent. He was a weapon.

The city was a mess. The building-explosion calendar had been delayed by a glycerin shortage. The first two supply attempts had ignited, causing enormous space-bombs that could be seen throughout the galaxy. But finally, an adequate supply had arrived on an Earth rocket. Now, with the opening of Mars By just hours away, the city was full of rubble, and truckloads of workers were frantically clearing it from the street and hauling it away. Meanwhile, other trucks were arriving, containing tents and portable sound systems and catering tables for the VIP hover-trailer food-materialization Courts, which would be spread throughout the city to give drunken VIPs sweet lounge relief from the tweaking masses. Down came an old building, up went VIP lounges for the enjoyment of people who'd never been to Mars before. They would have an awesome time at Mars By with their drink tickets, and then they'd go home to Earth and talk about what an awesome time they'd had. Then up would go a condo tower on the site of the tents, and it was always sold out by the time the solar windows got installed. Everyone wanted to have their own piece of Mars, a nice pad to hang in during Mars By.

The skies were full of honking pedi-trucks, which made quite a cacophony when mixed with the constant whine of the synthetic polymer-flooring dispensers. Jordan watched impassively as a group of men hitched themselves to an enormous slab of ancient Martian adobe and dragged it onto a cart, like slaves of old. They deposited the slab and stood there, panting.

Their supervisor came up to them. "Let's go," he said. "Three more slabs we gotta get up."

"We're thirsty," said one of the workers. "Give us some water."

"You want some water?" the supervisor said.

"Yes, please."

"I'll give you some water."

He shot the worker in the head. "*Anyone else want some water?*"

No one did. Mars was a right-to-work planet. That means you had the right to work if you wanted to. If you didn't work, people could kill you. That was *their* right.

Jordan had pledged to protect this fine system.

Not that he had any great affection for it; he didn't have any affection for anything. Crystal Waters had scrubbed his soul clean with rough lays and mind-altering drugs and endless, violent hologrammatic scenarios. She had transformed him into a sexy killer automaton of the state. The naïve young man he'd once been lay far beneath, under layers of confusion and muscle and bitterness and the known universe's most advanced battle armor.

"Look out below!" Jordan heard.

He instinctively twitched to the left and rolled. A huge chunk of polymer had fallen off the top of a ten-story building, and Jordan watched it crash to the dome floor just across the street from him.

The dome floor started to crack.

"Clear the perimeter!" the same voice shouted. "Atmospheric leak!"

There was a wailing siren. An enormous hover-truck appeared overhead. Three men in full hazmat gear dropped down from the truck on cords, each of them wielding a portable polymer cannon.

Jordan clambered up onto a ledge and crouched. These were the situations for which he trained. Not the leak, that was the work of the specialists who were being dropped. No, he had to watch for anarchists or revolutionaries. They liked to exploit situations like this. To them, an atmosphere leak was an opportunity. Dozens could die, and it would prove that the revolution had been right all along. If people like that showed up to make things worse, Jordan was going to take them out hard.

The specialists dropped and opened up the cannons. The crack was sealed within seconds. One of the workers later died from atmosphere exposure, but his family was adequately compensated with a hundred thousand credits and time-share use of a condo on Phobos. Disaster had been averted.

Jordan put on a nondescript jacket and walked out into traffic, senses tingling for trouble. All about him, New Austin buzzed for its big moment, the three months a year when it could showcase what it was and what corporations wanted it to be. The air was thrumming with music and energy and smelling like grain alcohol. Jordan stepped into the back of a tent. The building that had previously stood there had been torn down early in the cycle.

On a stage, a band was playing a final rehearsal before setting up for a three-month, 250-set Mars By. This was a new Earth band, on their first visit to Mars By. The Mars kids had been watching this band for months on their Devices. These preview gigs were the only ones that they actually got to attend. Most of the Mars By shows were VIP only, and the public shows were so big and so crowded and so expensive that teenagers, the real music fans, didn't get very close to the action. These free rehearsals were the only chance they had.

There were seven people in the band: a singer, two guitar players, a bassist, a drummer, a horn player, and a keyboard player. They all wore shiny red jumpsuits.

"Hello," the singer said. "We're the Critters, and we're from Earth."

Three perfect chords sounded out, and then a blissful melody exploded from the keyboard. The drummer started up, and the kids went crazy. They knew this song.

The crowd started bobbing up and down. Mars By had begun. Jordan listened to the music. Inside, his old self stirred, like a long-dormant larva. This music was beautiful, so bright, so optimistic, so communal, so . . . Earth.

There, everyone was the same skin color. Everyone spoke the same sixty languages. Everyone had Enough, and they made beautiful music in harmony. New Austin, and all of Mars, was a skanky hell-pit, a real-estate swindle. Jordan remembered his life on Earth—the kids he'd taught, his mother, those happy days strolling along the beach after work with his darling Daril by his side, the happy birds of the Earth singing just like this.

Tears slid down Jordan Kincaid's cheeks as he remembered who he really was.

A rocket screamed over Jordan's head, hit the stage, and exploded. Mars by Mars had begun.

26

The stage collapsed. Then the tent collapsed. People were screaming and writhing in blood, scratching for their lives inside a canvas cocoon. Some would survive and were definitely going to ask for a refund on their wristband fees.

But the Critters were roadkill. Jordan could see that, even through the smoke. They had come all the way from Earth to show the galaxy that they could rock, and instead their dreams, like their guts, lay splattered all over the stage. What kinds of monsters would murder such a beautiful band? Jordan was going to find out.

He stepped out of the tent perimeter and activated every Device he had. The infrared lens in his goggles could detect any heat level in any movement within two miles. His earpiece was attuned to any one of ten thousand vibrations. A massive tracking computer whirled on his wrist. No movement would go undetected.

Ignoring the chaos directly in front of him—hard to do, since people were flailing about, screaming—Jordan turned forty-five degrees to the right. Energy and data there were spilling away from the crowd at a pace fast enough that it was pretty obvious they'd bailed the very second of the explosion, if not just before it.

Emergency hovercraft hustled toward the flames, making the scene louder and more chaotic. But it wasn't Jordan's job to help or to clean up. It was his job to bring down the hammer.

He leapt onto his hover-pedi and launched himself toward the escaping streams. It was a first-class pedi, which meant he could go to the upper lanes, where traffic was a myth. Only peasants and terrorists got delayed. According to Jordan's training, the two were the same thing.

Up top, he slapped on the turbo and rocketed forward, leaving a thick, oxygen-rich vapor trail. Sometimes Jordan imagined flying up through the top of the dome, out into the universe, onward forever, away from all this madness. But most of the time he just chewed cannabis gum and waited to bust heads.

He saw them.

Three figures were scrambling on foot through the old market section, which the MDC had carefully preserved for filming by Earth documentarians. It was the quaintest and most authentic neighborhood in New Austin, two alleys of cheap trinkets and bad soup vendors curated in rigid touristic amber. It was the worst place to flee in the city. Pots were clanging everywhere. Jordan saw someone run flat into a fruit cart.

He swooped down. When he was about twenty feet high, he grabbed the handlebars of his hover-pedi, pushed down, and launched himself off the bike. It was a triple-gainer. He landed on the shoulders of one of the runners, clamped his thighs tight, and twisted to the left. The man's neck snapped immediately. He collapsed. Jordan crouched by his corpse.

Again he tuned into his Devices. He picked up the other two bodies, moving in separate directions. There was no way he could get to both. He moved to his left, swung up on an awning, and crashed into a basket of plaster Gaia totems. Jordan scooped one up, stood in the middle of the alley, and hurled Mother Earth at the back of a runaway skull. It connected. The woman crumpled.

Jordan was there in seconds. He flipped her over. She was still breathing. Her eyes opened. She spat in his face. He slapped her.

"Who are you?" he said.

"You know who I am," she said.

"Actually, I have no idea."

"Oh, well," she said.

And she spat in his face again.

He slapped her again.

"There are at least fifty dead people back there."

"Good," she said. "Maybe then Mars by Mars will stop coming in and taking away our land."

He pulled out his stunner. "Who sent you?" he said. "And where are they?"

"Captain Ted sends his regards," she said, and bit down hard.

Jordan had a split second to activate his body shield, and it was barely enough. The bubble formed around him as the girl exploded, sending him flying into a stand that sold bottled fermented soybean oil. He hit the glass with force, shattering it everywhere, which released an unusually foul odor.

Jordan crouched back, stunned, and retched at the hideous smell. He was unhurt, or at least as unhurt as he was after an average training session. There was a huge hole in the dome where the woman had blown herself apart. The people who could fled quickly for sealed-in areas. It usually took only 30 seconds or less for the dome to auto-repair. But sometimes it took a little longer depending on the severity of the breach, and then people started freezing. Jordan activated his filter just in case.

From above, he heard a roar. A giant sports-utility hover-pedi appeared in the air and settled beside him. Crystal Waters stepped out of the rear seat.

"Jordan, darling," she said. "Are you hurt?"

"I'm never hurt," Jordan said.

"That's my man," she said. "This is a terrible day."

"It is for me," Jordan said.

"For all of us," she said. "This wasn't even a little bar bomb. It was a major attack. On an *Earth band.* Do you know how much it's going to cost us to bribe people to keep this news from getting back to Earth?"

"I wouldn't mind going back to Earth myself," he said.

"Don't be ridiculous," she said.

She pulled him close and pressed her mouth against his. There was a premium vitamin tab on her tongue. It dissolved in his mouth before he could spit it out. Instantly, she had his heart and mind again.

"You are staying right here with me," she said.

"OK," said Jordan.

"Daddy wants to see you."

27

Dick Waters sat in his penthouse office, the highest point in all of New Austin, and looked out over the city he'd built. He counted six fires. One was an entire block long. Even though he had quadruple-paned soundproofed windows, he could still hear the sirens. If he strained, he could even hear the screaming.

"I worked thirty years for this shit," he said.

But no one was listening, not even the robot that fitted his toupee.

The door slid open.

"What?" he said.

"It's rough out there, Daddy," said Crystal Waters.

"I can see that," said Dick Waters.

He turned around. Crystal looked fresh as a spring morning. Next to her was Jordan, filthy, his armor studded with shrapnel.

"You were supposed to stop this from happening," Waters said.

"It was kind of sudden," Jordan said. "And I'm only one person."

"I'm not paying you—"

"That's right, you're *not* paying me."

Waters looked at Kincaid, who could have snapped his neck as easily as sliding a lugnut off a collapsible event platform, and decided not to press the situation.

There was another explosion below. Another half of a city block was set ablaze.

"Gaia damn it, this has got to stop!" Waters said. He looked at Jordan. "Are you going to stop it?"

"Not by myself," Jordan said. "These people are all over the place."

"Where are my security forces?"

"Daddy, there are thousands of extra people in the central city, and they are at hundreds of parties. There's absolutely no way to tell which one of them is carrying ordnance. Mars by Mars is huge."

Waters stood, his face red, his neck wattles flapping madly. "Cancel the whole fucking festival!" he bellowed.

"I was going to suggest the same thing. Of course . . ."

"It's going to cost us two trillion credits."

"Yes."

"Now we'll only have eighty trillion credits left."

"Right."

"If this happens forty more years in a row, we're fucked."

"It won't happen forty more years," she said. "In forty years, everyone who did this will be dead."

"I want them dead in forty *hours*!" Dick Waters said.

"Yes, Daddy," Crystal said. "But we're going to have to find them first."

♦ ♦ ♦

In the skies, a couple of levels above the city but not high enough to get the hell away from it, Leonard Tolliver hovered on his pedi. Two Earthlings screamed in the backseat, as they'd been doing for a half hour.

"Let us off, let us off!" one of them howled.

"It's not safe," Leonard said.

"We have to get back to our vacation rental!"

"I'm trying."

"It's costing us three thousand credits a night, and it's twenty-five minutes from downtown. I told you to check a map, Gary. And now we're stuck in an über-pedi. During surge pricing! What a rip-off."

"Lady," Leonard said, "if I were you right now, I'd be *glad* I'm staying twenty-five minutes from downtown, whatever the cost. It is hell down there, and it's getting worse."

He knew the truth. As soon as he dropped off these terrified tourists, he was scheduled to fire a triple-shelled grenade into the heart of the Mangapus Showcase Stage. It was one of sixteen attacks still scheduled. Captain Ted had called for thirty, one for each year of Mars by Mars. Leonard honestly didn't know if he was going to go through with it. He had never killed anyone before and didn't relish the idea of assassinating innocent fans of the galaxy's greatest holographic cartoon.

"We have to land!" the woman said.

"I need to get you back home," Leonard said. "No one should be walking down there."

Almost directly below them, an explosion sounded. It knocked the pedi sideways. Leonard wasn't that good at steering in a normal circumstance. The flipping holographic dials and warning lights distracted him. He let go of the bars. The side-shield went up, but it was too late. Leonard bashed hard into the pedi in the lane next to him. A flaming polymer shard shot up from below. It nearly split the pedi in half. Leonard's passengers were really screaming now.

"Put it down!" said the man. "Put this thing down now!"

Leonard didn't see a parking spot anywhere in his field. The shard had disrupted his pedi's Device. The pedi was sputtering and streaming hydrogen smoke.

But it still worked. Leonard lowered the smoking pedi down as gently as he could, half sideways, next to a red curb. But there was no way the MDC was going to enforce parking rules during this chaos.

He looked behind him. His passengers didn't seem like they were hurt.

"That'll be twenty-seven hundred credits," Leonard said.

"Fuck you!" said the guy.

"Sorry," Leonard said. "Surge pricing."

They left without paying their fare, running off terrified into the flame-tinged night, their awesome trip to Mars by Mars totally ruined. Leonard, meanwhile, had to figure out how to get back to base. He recognized a child of the rebellion running past him, grinning hard.

"Hey!" he shouted.

"Victory now, my brother!" the rebel shouted back at him.

Leonard didn't have much time for slogans, but this guy was probably heading toward a pedi stashed in a garage somewhere, which would get Leonard back to his bunk and a fresh supply of Space Cakes.

"Victory now," Leonard said.

"We just torched the Tranquility Showcase," the guy said proudly.

"Yeah?"

"Yeah, people are fucked up," the guy said.

"Where was the security?"

"Nowhere," the guy said. "I think we're winning!"

"I doubt that." Leonard had seen what the MDC security forces could do.

"Can you give me a lift to the depot?" the guy asked.

"We're gonna have to hoof," Leonard said, pointing toward the damaged pedi. A parking cop was there, giving him a ticket.

Fuck the MDC.

The security forces, or at least the best of them, gathered in the basement of MDC headquarters. Dick Waters had pulled his people off the streets, letting the municipal squads and fire crews handle the chaos on the ground. He didn't hire and train his top mercenaries to use extinguishers and pick tourists out of the rubble.

A hundred or so heavily armored militia, Jordan Kincaid among them, stood around, looking nervous. Waters faced them, at front of the room, Crystal behind him. He didn't seem happy.

"The rebels just broadcast this message broadcast to every Device on Mars," he said. "'People of New Austin,'" he read aloud, "'Mars by Mars is over. The MDC isn't in charge anymore. This is a new era for Mars, an era of the people. No longer will the MDC be allowed to—' I can't do this. I can't even talk."

Dick Waters had to sit down. This whole thing was making him feel tired and old. He had built a great city in space, and now they were going to blow it up. For what? To prove some point? Because they didn't work hard enough to afford their own apartments?

Crystal took over.

"Look," she said. "They can declare all property law nullified all they want, but we all know that they are not going to be able to seize control of the central district, much less make all hotels communally owned and distribute their furniture equally. It's just nonsense. We have more soldiers and more weapons. Not many people on Mars are going to put up with this crap for long. I've got the numbers. They have attacked eight stages so far. Medical staff is counting fifty-four dead and a few hundred injured, most of those minor. That's several hundred families that are going to be on our side, not the rebels'."

"So what do we do?" said a soldier. "We can guard every stage, but they're totally blended in."

"We've canceled the festival," Crystal said.

The security people murmured approval. None of them enjoyed standing around all week watching Earthpeople get wasted. And few of them actually enjoyed music. For them, Mars by Mars was just a three-month hassle.

"Not permanently," she said.

That shut them up.

"But for this year, at least, it's off. I'm going to need a dozen of you at the spaceport because there are going to be emergency bailouts left and right. We're going to have ten rockets flying out of here every day for a month. Any volunteers?"

No hands went up.

"OK," she said. "We'll pick at random. The rest of you are going to lead squads to attack rebel headquarters."

"Um, I'll do the spaceport," a voice said from the back.

"Too late," she said. "You get to head up the first line of attack."

"Dangit."

"Now we just have to figure out where we're going."

From his chair, Dick Waters said, "I want Captain Ted dead! Dead, I tell you! I want you to tear out his fucking guts and tie them around his neck, and I will hang him from the top of this tower and let the vulture-robots lick his bones. Let this be a warning to you all; no one fucks with the MDC!"

"Someone get Daddy his medicine," said Crystal Waters.

Jordan's Device pinged. Not the one the MDC had given him, but his personal one, which never pinged because no one on Mars except for Crystal knew him from before. No one except . . .

He pulled the Device out of his pocket.

Leonard.

28

Leonard sat in the back of a stolen hover-pedi. The rebel driving it smelled like stale beer and cheap weed and dried seaweed and generally poor sanitary habits.

"This is the greatest day in the history of the universe," the rebel said.

Leonard doubted that. They hovered in chaotic traffic, hoping no one shot them down with a stationary rocket. Emergency craft sped past, fires blazed, people screamed. The rebel chuckled. Leonard had trouble seeing how this scene could give anyone pleasure. To his eyes, the revolution seemed to be nothing but disaster porn for excitement junkies.

Outside of the downtown core, things quieted. The MDC had built the city large, but the outlying neighborhoods—the nice ones with the pet boutiques and the medical-marijuana clinics and the tasteful restaurants serving butter-poached Luna veal and organically farmed otter steaks with chili verde salsa—represented the real key to Martian prosperity. Here, calm-looking homes spread over a third of an acre, landscaped with plants imported from Arizona and Spain, interspersed with low-lying, two-block apartment buildings, all of which had yoga studios and coffee breweries and hydrogen inflato-bars on the ground level. The orthopedists and orthodontists and orthotic mattress designers came here after work. Downtown may have been weird once, but now it was just a trap. And the rebels had certainly trapped people there.

These neighborhoods are nice, Leonard thought, not for the first time. *I wouldn't mind living in one of them myself.*

Ninety-five percent of Mars had nothing to do with the festival. Most of the workers came in from other planets, as did most of the attendees. So who did Captain Ted think he was going to bring down?

As they reached the limits of the developed area, Leonard and his ride turned off their Devices. They didn't want the MDC tracking them to the wretched former public-housing towers that the rebellion called home. They could feel the winds from outside. The dust choked everything. Most of New Austin didn't have these problems. For a few square miles, the people reigned, and they were disgusting.

Leonard walked into the lobby of the central tower. A group of sniveling anarchists were piling chairs onto a fire. The lobby filled with smoke and the discordant three-chord riff, endlessly repeated, of "Fuck the MDC." A few sad children, their faces smeared with red dirt, squirted in and out of the room, looking ragged and possibly drunk. Their parents, whoever they were, hadn't yet determined where the kids fit into the new Martian order.

All around the town, the MDC's going down, went the song.

Leonard took the stairs, because the elevators hadn't worked in fifteen years. He wrapped a bandana around his face, because the stairwell smelled like piss and shit and discarded needles and rotting food and probably dead animals. It reeked of death and decay and horror.

Little hands were reaching up through the iron stair bars, grasping for the scraps of food they hoped Leonard might be carrying. This society was going to challenge the MDC and their eighty-trillion-credit surplus? Leonard had more than his share of doubts.

Up the stairs he went. Sure, the people owned them communally, but where were the repairs? Every third step was missing or completely beyond saving. Years of soot and graffiti covered the walls, and lighting was reserved for people who could afford generators in their apartments. Leonard was glad he had a headlamp. Otherwise, he wouldn't have seen the bodies he had to step over. He wondered how many of them were alive.

Captain Ted sat atop the tower, like the king of the chimpanzee exhibit at the zoo. He had his own bathroom and kitchen, plus three other rooms all to himself: a bedroom, a room for him to practice his guitar, and a living room that he called the "command center." He lived here, at the pinnacle of the housing projects, when he wasn't letting people buy him drinks at the Black Pig. He didn't occupy the highest point in New Austin—there were lots of buildings downtown that were higher—but he was up top as far as this neighborhood was concerned.

Leonard had clearance to enter. The guards let him through. Captain Ted stood at his triple-paned windows, which he'd had installed at considerable expense, and watched the smoke from the city rise from miles away. The room was plastered with posters for events featuring bands that Leonard had never heard of, memories of a time that rocked, when the city was shitty and the world was young.

Captain Ted saw Leonard's reflection in the glass.

"Report, Tolliver," he said.

"It's a fucking mess out there, Captain Ted."

"I can see that. But what's the news from the ground?"

"People are screaming. There's lots of blood. I think they've canceled the festival."

"It's begun."

"What's begun?"

"The end of the MDC. The end of an era. The end of Mars by Mars. Of what I should have ended before it started. But I'm wondering why they're not fighting back."

"You caught them by surprise," Leonard said. "They didn't expect this to happen to the city."

"I did. When I came here, Tolliver, I just wanted to build. It worked fine on Earth—a little boring, maybe, because the codes were so rigid, but it was effective. You built things, and people lived and worked in them their entire lives. But not Mars. There's a property cycle. It's in the plan; I've seen it. You think this is going to last? It's not going to last. We're getting close to Peak Mars. Cheap investment money is going to pour into this city like it's an open sewer drain, and then the bubble is going to pop. When that happens, this shit-hole we're living in is going to seem like a luxury hotel. Build and destroy, build and destroy. People have to stand by and take it like an enema. But maybe they don't."

"What are you going to do?"

"Burn it down," Captain Ted said. "All of it. That's all it deserves."

"There are five million people down there, Captain. They're not all bad."

"There were one million people when I got here, and they weren't all bad, either. Where are they now?"

"Most of them are still here," Leonard said. "Some of them probably died. Of old age. Not in fires."

"They died refugees on the planet where they were born. I saw them vaporized."

"Look, I'm not saying this is an easy debate, but—"

"There's no more debating, Tolliver. Do you think Dick Waters wants to *debate* you? He wants your money and your land and nothing else, and I am not going to let him have it."

Leonard didn't have much money, and he *certainly* didn't have any land, but Captain Ted didn't tolerate dissent any more than Dick Waters did.

"By the time I'm done, Dick Waters isn't going to have any city left to tear down. He's going to have to rebuild from scratch. And that is not his specialty."

"People are going to suffer," Leonard said.

"People *always* suffer! That's what people do. Are you losing your nerve, Tolliver?"

"No, Captain."

"Good." He lit a joint, puffed it, and passed it over to Leonard, who accepted. Leonard never turned down weed. Not even from a madman.

Captain Ted's shit was strong. The strongest. He'd developed a strain that grew well in Martian soil. It clouded judgment and opened the brain up to the possibilities of the universe.

Seconds passed, or maybe minutes, or possibly hours. Captain Ted looked out over the landscape and liked what he saw. Leonard didn't feel the same way.

"We're going to blow up MDC headquarters, Tolliver," Captain Ted said. "The whole fucking thing."

"When?"

"Soon. And you're going to be there."

The Martian ditch weed had just made Leonard's thinking clearer: he had to get the hell off Mars, and quickly. This whole city was set to blow, and he didn't see a way to stop it from happening.

"I need to grab some dinner first," Leonard said.

"Yeah, that's fine," said Captain Ted. "I've still got some plans to sketch."

He didn't have plans that Leonard could see, other than total anarchy. Is that what he wanted? Wasn't there some sort of middle ground?

There was a ladder leading to the roof. Leonard took what was left of Captain Ted's joint and climbed up. He pulled out his Device and stared at it for a minute. Then he deactivated the cloaking function and pressed on a familiar face icon.

Seconds later, Jordan's head filled the screen.

"Hey, buddy," Jordan said. "It's been a while. I thought you were dead."

"Not yet," Leonard said. "What about you?"

"I'm talking to you, right?"

"Right. You been doing drugs?"

"Too many," said Jordan. "Crystal is an animal."

"Good for you, dude. But are you aware of what's going on out there?"

"Crazy stuff," Jordan said.

"Are you staying safe?"

"I'm fine. What about you?"

"Fine for now. But listen, man, we've got to get out of here. I don't know how we're going to do that. But it's going to get a lot worse. We've got to get on one of those rockets."

"I agree," Jordan said.

There was a long pause. They hadn't talked to each other in months.

"I have to go back to work now."

"Me, too," Leonard said. "What are you doing?"

"Can't talk about it."

"Me, either.

"OK. Be in touch, man."

"You, too," Leonard said.

He hung up. Jordan had looked good. Maybe a little thick around the neck. But really good overall. They'd figure a way out of this place together.

He took another puff of Super Martian Haze. Such a beautiful city, such a beautiful planet. Such a shame that it was such a shit-hole.

♦ ♦ ♦

Jordan had ducked outside of the meeting room at MDC headquarters. He came back in. Dick Waters was still snarling on stage.

"You better have a good excuse, son," he said. "No one leaves when I'm talking!"

Jordan crossed his arms and stared at Waters calmly. This man didn't intimidate him. No one did.

"I know where they are," he said.

29

Dick Waters pounded his fist. It hit the invisible plexi-desk and bounced back up. He looked surprised. His mouth constricted into an enraged snarl. Crystal stood in front of him, waiting for him to burn out. Jordan was by the door, arms crossed.

"I want them fucking dead!" Waters said. "All of them! I want you to roll out all the sonic cannons and vaporize their buildings and everything inside! I don't want anything left. Not their hair. Not their skin. Not their shit-stained gutterpunk assholes!"

Crystal looked at him impassively. "There are women in those buildings," she said. "Probably hundreds of them."

"Who cares about women?" Waters said. "You think women can't carry a gun? You think women can't set things on fire? They have to die. All of them!"

"Children, then."

"Children, too. They can do a lot of damage if you train them right. Look at what happened to you."

"Fine," Crystal said. "Then babies. There are almost certainly babies. Daddy, do you want to be known as the man who ended the rebellion by killing babies? How do you think that's going to play on Earth Devices?

"I'll tell you how it'd play. Badly. Luxury time-share rentals are going to go down seventy percent, and we're going to have to host a bunch of backpackers. Adventure travelers don't spend any money. We don't want them. And if we don't have the luxury temporary-housing crowd, that will create a housing surplus."

"That's the last thing I fucking want!"

"Right now," Crystal said, "we have the moral high ground, which is something the MDC hasn't occupied in a very long time. The resistance blew up a dozen stages, killed seventy-five people, eradicated three-quarters of a popular Earth band, and hospitalized at least two hundred more. You know what they call that on Earth? Terrorism. People don't care what the terrorists are rebelling against. They don't care that Mars is unaffordable for three out of every four people who live here, or that a rasher of GMO bacon costs three hundred thousand credits. Most people—even most people on Mars—are going to look at their Devices and say, 'What the fuck is wrong with these terrorists?'"

"So let's kill 'em!" Waters said.

"If you go in and vaporize a half dozen towers—towers that *you helped build*—you are going to look like a monster. We don't want to build sympathy for the other side."

Dick Waters pouted like a grumpy old baby. "I don't care," he said. "I want them down."

"Also," Crystal said, "people still own the towers communally. It's the last real estate in New Austin that's grandfathered in under the original settlement clause."

"That was"—Waters made air quotes—"*Captain Ted's* idea," he snarled.

"Regardless of whose idea it was, it's still the law, and unless you want Earth inspectors coming here and slapping down fines and asking to look at our files—"

"I would sooner burn this city to the ground than have Earth bureaucrats looking through my personal finance files," Waters said. "That's why I left Earth in the first place!"

"I figured you would say that," said Crystal.

"What do you suggest?"

"We know where they are now," she said. "And we've got the city on lockdown. Unless they want to start standing in empty streets and firing rockets at random buildings, we've tamped down the rebellion. I think we should marshal our forces, all of them, and go down to the towers and wait. If they start shooting, *then* we have the pretext to attack. We do not want to seem like the aggressors."

"What about the children?" Waters said sneeringly. "Won't someone think about the children?"

"There's a difference between murder and collateral damage."

"Is there?" Jordan said.

"Shut up, Kincaid," said Dick Waters. "You're not being paid for your opinions."

"I'm not being paid at all."

"You're gonna be dead!"

"Just try it, old man."

"Now, boys, put away your dick-swords," said Crystal. "Jordan and you are *both* right to be concerned. We're going to intimidate them out of hiding. Hopefully they will be smart enough to surrender, or at least to send away the most vulnerable people. But we all know that Captain Ted has an itchy trigger finger. He's been waiting a long time for this. Once they fire on us, then we can attack. By the time we're done bombing, the buildings will be so damaged that we'll *have* to tear them down and redevelop the land."

"I like the way you think, girl," Waters said.

"I'm no girl."

That she wasn't. Crystal Waters had been raised for this moment. While her brother, David, had spent his childhood staring at himself in the mirror, or playing with his holographic Mangapus figurines, she'd been playing galactic chess with her father, learning how to think three, six, nine steps ahead. In primary school, they called her the "Bug Squasher," because that's what she did, squash bugs and make people eat them. But then somehow she'd always persuade the faculty and students that this was in the best interests of the school. Where other people would get suspended, she'd get rewarded. Back on Earth, she was first in her class in the Kigali Leadership Academy—a place only the top 1 percent of the top 1 percent of galactic students got to attend—a rank she'd achieved by seducing the janitor to get hold of test materials, but also by stealing the test materials digitally. She was a double cheater. And she got caught, on purpose. She denied the theft, and the administration made her take another test, by herself, triple-blind, which she passed with a perfect score. Later, she told the administration that she'd cheated to expose holes in their system. Not only did she manage to get herself named valedictorian, she got herself placed on the school's payroll, permanently. Her father gave a 970-million-credit endowment, one-tenth of which was for the MDC Chair in Corporate Responsibility, which she occupied in perpetuity. Once every three years, she went to Earth for a month, gave the same five holographic lectures, and returned home a laurelled academic.

Crystal always knew all the answers, because she'd already written all the questions.

"So are we good, Daddy?" she asked.

"We're fine."

"We'd better be," she said. "So let's stop talking and roll out the cannons."

She turned on her heels and headed for the door.

"Time for our nap, Jordan," she said.

"But I'm not tired," Jordan said.

"Good," she said. "Because we're not going to be sleeping."

30

Eighteen days passed. The Earthpeople left. Some had permanent injuries, most had terrible stories, but all had generous settlements. The next year's Mars By crew wasn't due in for at least three months. All the clubs and restaurants remained silent. Central New Austin shut down at night like the Main Street of a fundie provincial capital. Slowly, the MDC began to restore order.

There were still attacks at night, but those were almost entirely from preteen copycat vigilantes, most armed with little more than stick guns. The squads knew how to deal with those kids. One broken finger and they'd never cross the MDC again.

Leonard pulled his hover-pedi up to the Black Pig and heard the rowdiness from inside.

What a bunch of assholes, he thought. *These people just don't realize the value of work.*

At that moment, Leonard realized that Mars had changed him.

This was the first time he'd ever had a job. He felt genuinely *proud* of it, even if 75 percent of his pay was going into a communal kitty that seemed mostly to pay for other people's liquor. He woke up in the morning, exercised for an hour, and then worked the rest of the day, with the exception of the three-hour midday lunch-nap-vape-video-game session. Balance was important. But even after that, Leonard usually put in four hours, give or take. Leonard had absorbed a touch of good old-fashioned Martian self-reliance, and he felt proud.

The revolution, on the other hand, had left him feeling more than a tad ambivalent. He believed that every Martian had the right to safe, clean, and affordable housing like people did on Earth. Some of the restaurants here were loud and pretentious and overpriced. But was the best solution really murdering hundreds of innocent people? Was that a war worth winning?

These questions haunted Leonard at the end of every shift. Now that the "Battle of Mars By" had sat for a week, he wondered if Captain Ted even had a plan, beyond pure anarchy. Maybe Leonard was just being a typically weak Earth liberal, obsessed with process and justice. Maybe this was how social change actually happened. Either way, he needed a drink.

He went inside. As soon as he opened the door, Leonard saw a guy slug half a bottle, grab a handful of THC Space Chips, shove them into his mouth, and slam his head against the table.

"Whooo!" he shouted. "Victory!"

The guy was wearing a leather jacket. It bore hundreds of metal studs, one each for the number of people killed in their rocket attacks. Also, he'd painted his face with thick clown makeup, complete with crazy, menacing grin, and had shaved his head into a Mohawk. He thought it was real badass.

"Fuck the MDC" played extra loudly. Leonard walked up to the bar.

"Double bourbon," he said. "Luna rocks."

"Seventeen credits," the bartender said.

"It was eight credits last week."

"Happy hour is over."

In revolutionary times, booze prices doubled. All hail the people's paradise. Leonard paid reluctantly.

He walked over to the idiot in the clown face and the Mohawk. When Leonard had come to Mars, this guy, whose named was Nickel, was wearing overalls and playing the banjo. This was a fashion change. Captain Ted turned everyone into his punk.

"Hey, Nickel," Leonard said.

"What you want, mate?" the guy said in a fake Cockney accent.

"I want to see Captain Ted."

"Oy, Captain Ted is busy right now, mate. He's busy fucking the girls and boys, right? To the victor goes the spoils, eh?" Nickel took a slug of bourbon, threw back his head, and laughed in his evil clown voice. "Eh heh heh heh heh heh heh!"

Leonard grabbed Nickel by the Mohawk, lifted his head up, and smashed it down on the table, not too hard. Nickel bounced back up quick, snuffling like a pig.

"Some of us are more spoiled than others," Leonard said.

He went upstairs. Captain Ted, as advertised, sat cross-legged on a mattress, watching as a sexy revolutionary lady and two sexy revolutionary gentlemen writhed in front of him, licking and sucking and blowing and slurping. The rebels went about their pleasure seeking with androgynous ruthlessness.

Captain Ted wore only a bandana of the Martian flag and a pair of filthy boxer-briefs. The room was loud and dank, and it reeked of crappy Martian ditch weed. The words "Mars Is for Bitches" had been spray-painted on the walls. Captain Ted's golden vision for the Red Planet had dawned.

"Tolliver!" he said, arms extended. "Join us!"

"No, I'm fine," Leonard said.

"Well, you can at least watch."

"It doesn't seem like I have any choice."

"It's a good show."

"I'm sure it is, Captain. Listen, I need to talk to you."

"Can it wait?"

"Not really. I don't know if you've seen the city out there, but it's a mess."

"I bet it is."

"I mean, people are wandering around in the streets. Their homes were destroyed. They don't have food or water or sanitation."

"That is the Martian way! We're bringing this city back to reality," Captain Ted said as the nubile, young revolutionary woman nibbled on his thighs.

"But the reality is that people are suffering."

"Doin' it Mars-style," Captain Ted. "Old school. When the MDC surrenders, Mars is going back to the people. Where it fuckin' belongs!"

"Captain, the MDC is not going to surrender. We need to be prepared."

"Bullshit!" Captain Ted said. "They can't stop us. They don't even know who we are!"

"We should be out there providing support," Leonard said. "Divert some of the booze money. Get people some water and tents, at least until this blows over."

Captain Ted looked at Leonard quizzically. "Are you suggesting a course of guilt-ridden bourgeois *humanitarianism*?"

"Um, no, just helping people," Leonard said. "That's all."

"How do you know what's good for them?"

"Food is good for most people," said Leonard. "Look, let's at least make an effort. It might make people a little more sympathetic to our cause."

"There is no cause," said Captain Ted.

"What?"

"Causes are for politicians. I'm done with causes."

Captain Ted gave a little gasp. A human plaything had just gone down on his ancient revolutionary member, which was engorged with black-market Mars Dust balm.

"We are free people on a free Mars," he said. "Are you going to fight for us?"

Leonard stood there, incredulously. "What choice do I have?" he said.

You are dismissed, Tolliver."

Leonard didn't move.

"Get out!" shouted Captain Ted.

Leonard went downstairs, where Nickel was still cackling mercilessly.

"Eh heh heh heh heh heh!"

Leonard walked up to the bar. "Two triple bourbons, neat," he said.

"Seventy-nine credits," said the bartender.

Leonard walked over to Nickel, picked him up by the shirt collar, and threw him against the jukebox. Finally, "Fuck the MDC" stopped playing.

"Charge it to the clown," he said, and walked out.

31

The revolution had gone underground. Jordan Kincaid was getting ready to make that situation permanent. Crystal had put him in charge. It would, she estimated, take two hundred elite ground troops, plus a phalanx of pedi-soldiers, plus five sonic cannon-tanks to bring the resistance to heel. They had more in reserve if necessary, but why waste resources?

The tanks rolled onto the floor of the MDC Amphitheater, which was supposed to, on this night, host the Martian debut of Antiseptic Cave Dwarves, Earth's biggest holographic music collective. But the Dwarves, having survived the attacks, were currently on a rocket back to Earth, enjoying full VIP privileges, which included memory-wash drugs designed for them to tell the press that Mars was awesome and the disturbances overblown by an activist media.

An army assembled in their stead.

Jordan stood in front of them, arms behind his back, impassively watching his troops assemble. They didn't impress him. Take away their fancy skin-hugging body armor and their high-end guns, and what were they? Nothing, just meat and bone, slaves to the company that paid their salaries. They had no conscience and even less ability.

"Company, rotate *left*!" he shouted.

The soldiers and tanks and hover-bikes moved in unison.

"Rotate *right*!"

They complied.

"Break it down with the shimmy shimmy!"

They stared at him impassively.

"That was a joke," he said.

"They don't get it," said a voice from behind him.

It was Crystal.

"We don't train our soldiers in Earth irony," she said.

"Maybe you should," Jordan said. "Maybe they'd think twice."

"Before what?" she said.

"Before killing people."

"Look," she said, "I'm not going to pretend that we're innocent in all this. I know that Daddy is a monster and that Mars has some problems that need addressing. But we are not out there *murdering*."

"Not yet."

"Does someone need a wafer?"

"No more mind control, Crystal," he said. "I've had my training. I know what I'm doing. I just miss it, my home."

"This is your home now."

"Home is where you pay rent."

"You can't afford the rent on Mars."

Jordan sighed. "On Earth," he said, "I taught people about history and literature and love and how to be a better human. Here, I just kill."

"You haven't killed too many yet," said Crystal.

Jordan looked out at his troops. "That's about to change," he said.

"Probably," she said, "but it's for the best. As soon as we can take care of things, we can get New Austin back to what it was like in the old days—really cool and laid back, with tolerance for all kinds of viewpoints. It's only tipped in the last three or four years."

"Everyone I talk to says it was better in the old days," Jordan said. "No matter which side they're on."

"It was," she said, "before terrorists were blowing up nightclubs. So let's bring those days back, what do you say?"

Jordan sighed. "Fine," he said. "Company! Move out!"

◆ ◆ ◆

'Twas the week after Mars By, and all through the streets of New Austin, not a creature was stirring, not even hovering delivery people in the service lanes. No one waited in line at restaurants or clubs. Everything had closed for the duration of the crisis. The city had even tamped down its glow, making the outline of the dome that enclosed it visible for the first time in years. As the sun dipped low, everything appeared eerily blue in the swirling dust. The illusion of modernity and safety evaporated.

Everyone could see that they were on an alien planet, millions of miles from anywhere good, and that they were alone. They stared into the night and pondered the wonders of infinity and the smallness of their hastily and shoddily constructed personalities. After a few minutes of that, they turned on their Devices and amused themselves with holograms.

Jordan had no such luxury. He needed to work; he hovered two byways above his legion, which was snaking through the streets in small platoons. They didn't want to call attention to the deployment. If they found out, the rebels would scurry like rats, and then they'd just be cannoning towers full of bastard babies.

His infragoggles had ten split screens. He could track all his troops on the micro level, but had the macro handled, too.

"What's the report?" Crystal said into his earpiece.

"It's dead out here," he said. "Everyone is hiding."

"Cowards," she said. "Keep moving."

That was the intention.

They were walking through narrow streets, the commercial district, where the towers went tall and the food stalls all closed after midnight. There had been some historic preservation over here, to the chagrin of developers, and it created a problem for patrols because there were dark places to hide among the gleam of corporate windows. To his left, in an alley a block behind Seventh Platoon, Jordan saw a flash.

"Platoon Seven!" he shouted. "About-face and drop!"

The soldiers whirled and hit the ground. A rocket blast smacked into the sonic cannon, blowing it to bits. The shockwave went upward and rocked two pedis off their courses. A pilot took shrapnel in his neck. His pedi whirled into the side of a building and exploded.

Jordan plunged downward, to the source of the cannon fire. At the end of an alley, he saw a body scrambling up an escape ladder. Jordan applied the afterthrusters, hovered above the ladder, and jumped off the bike onto a platform directly above the man on the ladder.

A man wearing a studded leather jacket, clown makeup, and a Mohawk haircut.

"What in Gaia's name?" Jordan said.

The clown drew a cannon. Jordan kicked it away, jumped down a level, grabbed the clown by the lapel, and shoved him against the wall. The clown shrieked.

"Who are you?"

"I am your worst nightmare," the clown said. "Eh heh heh heh heh heh!"

Jordan slapped him. "Try again. How many of you are there? Why are you doing this? Who is in charge?"

"We're gonna bring it down. All of it. We're gonna bring back the old New Austin."

Jordan hit the clown, and again, and again. Now there was blood on the makeup.

A couple of hover-soldiers had caught up.

"Take this idiot to a basement cell," Jordan said. "One with lots of bugs."

"You can't intimidate us," the clown said.

"Watch me," Jordan said. "I'm coming for you and all your friends."

"You'll never stop them. Eh heh heh heh heh heh!"

Jordan threw a kick at the clown's head.

That shut him up.

32

Leonard burst into the lobby of the main tower, panic in his eyes.

"They're coming!" he said.

There were two junkies sitting in the lobby, completely insensate, with liquid Mars Dust drop-bottles scattered around them.

"Whuuuuuu?" one of them said.

"The MDC is coming!"

"The MDC what?"

Where *was* everyone? Usually, they had armed guards, two each outside and inside the main door, with sentry snipers scattered throughout the balcony. Every floor had a security guard as well. But now the towers seemed completely empty and unguarded. The lights flickered on and off in the lobby. Graffiti covered the walls. It stank of shit and death.

From down the hallway, Leonard could hear a baby wailing. He walked down the hall and knocked on the door.

A young woman answered. Well, she might have been young, but her face looked sallow and exhausted. She had a dirty, emaciated baby in her arms and a filthy toddler straddling her leg.

"What, mister?" she said.

"You have to get out!" said Leonard. "They are coming."

"Who's coming?" she said.

"The MDC."

"So?"

"So they want to kill us!"

"Why?"

"You don't know?"

"Mister, I have these two babies in here, and I never leave the apartment 'cept to take out the trash."

"It's on the news! The footage!"

"I haven't been able to watch my Device in years. When I moved in here, they said it was going to be free, but it's never worked."

"Goddamn it," Leonard said. "You have to get out."

"Man, I got nowhere to go," she said. "I'm gonna die here." She paused and looked upward. "Hopefully soon."

"Oy."

"You got any food, mister?"

Leonard had a bag of chips and a two-hundred-credit food coupon in his bag. "Here," he said.

She looked at the coupon like she couldn't believe it. And then she slammed the door in Leonard's face.

"You're welcome," he said.

Things hadn't been glamorous when Sonia was alive, but at least people had been clean. She kept people organized. The water ran and crews cleaned up the trash. A semblance of civil society existed, a hint of a Mars where everyone had Enough. Babies didn't starve. Now Captain Ted was totally in charge, and it had all gone to shit.

He went back out into the lobby.

"*Is anybody here?*" he shouted.

The junkies were there, but they just moaned.

"Gaia, help us," said Leonard.

Where was everybody? The MDC tanks were maybe twenty minutes away.

He went outside. There, he saw one of the dudes he knew, who was loading a keg of beer into his hover-pedi.

"What's going on?" Leonard said. "We've got to rally up and protect people."

"Whatever."

"There are like five tanks coming our way, and a shit-ton of soldiers."

"That's bullshit," the guy said.

"Man, it is all *over* your Devices. They are coming to exterminate us."

"No way, Captain Ted says the war is already won. We killed hundreds of yuppies!"

Leonard stared at him in disbelief.

"Victory for the people! Party at the Black Pig!"

The guy got on his pedi and sped away.

Suddenly, Leonard realized: *I'm on the wrong side.*

♦ ♦ ♦

Jordan's troops were within range of the towers. There were seven, all in tremendous disrepair—big chunks of plaster missing, shattered balconies, graffiti, creeping vines. The buildings looked ruined, abandoned, a left-behind warning from a lost civilization. This place didn't look fit for cave rats to shit in, much less house a sophisticated terror army.

"Halt!" Jordan shouted.

The parade of soldiers stopped. It was quiet out there on the prairie. Only the dark winds from outside, relentlessly beating against the

Permadome, made a sound. Jordan heard someone at the end of the line cough. That's how quiet it was.

"Advance!" he said.

The platoons, once they'd gotten outside of the populated areas, had merged into a broad phalanx, not too concentrated, ready to spread out farther or enact a pincer movement, depending on the needs of the situation. About a third of the troops had been sent to circle over from the left, in case reinforcements proved necessary.

At the moment, it seemed like two or three kids with slingshots would have been enough to take the towers. *Where is everybody?* Jordan wondered. The line moved forward again, slowly, carefully. Now they were just a few hundred yards from the towers. They moved through a concrete parking lot now, having to avoid a rusted-out pedi here or there, but nothing stronger than a plastic bag came at them.

"Halt!" Jordan said again.

The line stopped.

"Wait here," he said. "Myers, move forward."

"Alone?" Myers said.

"What, are you afraid?" said Jordan.

"Why should I be?"

"Exactly. So move it."

Myers's hover-pedi crept forward a hundred feet or so. Then more. Myers turned around.

"There's no one h—"

A sonic shot pinged from a high floor. Myers's helmet cracked open. The bullet ripped through his cheekbone and out his jaw. He fell off the pedi, screaming.

There was a pause in the ranks. Jordan raised his right arm as if to tell them to wait. But then from the back he heard the cry.

"*Kill them all!*"

The soldiers charged forward, screaming "*Yaaaaaaaah!*" They were heavily armored. The tanks followed behind and the hover-pedis zipped above. On the ground, the soldiers were shooting hundreds of rounds of automatic ammo into the lobby. Above, the pedi pilots were firing rockets into the floors. Before they even got to the entrances, three of the five towers were on fire.

"Wait!" Jordan shouted into his Device. "Halt! Wait! There's no one firing at us."

It was true. His infragoggles weren't picking up anything coming from the building. Whatever knocked out Myers had been one shot. Whoever perched in those towers didn't have anything to match what Jordan was throwing at them.

"I said cease fire! Cease fire immediately!"

Now the commandos were at the building, busting in the front door, smashing out windows, firing indiscriminately inside. It had been a stressful month. Also, despite a lot of hologram training, they hadn't actually faced real combat. This was certainly Jordan's first battle.

Except it wasn't a battle at all.

Jordan walked into the entryway. The guns had crisped it good. The foundations seemed crumbling and unsafe, though it was high odds that they'd already been that way. Two bodies, a couple of shabby junkies who wouldn't have had the strength or resources to squash a cockroach, lay among the rubble, ruined and bloody.

Still, throughout the hallway, Jordan could hear guns blazing, soldiers shouting.

He sounded the emergency "stand down" siren. It sent a crippling electronic signal through every helmet and disabled every weapon. His soldiers dropped to their knees, clutching their helmets. He'd stopped them more effectively than any enemy force could.

Jordan stood in the foyer. It smelled like death, and he didn't really sense too many dead people. Death had been making its home in this building for a long time.

A soldier—one of the stronger ones—staggered out of a hallway holding his head.

"Why'd you do that?" he said. "We were winning."

Behind him stood a young woman who nonetheless looked very old.

"Do you have any food for my baby, mister?" she said.

She was cradling the bloodied corpse of a newborn.

Suddenly, Jordan realized: *I'm on the wrong side.*

Outside, he heard the whine of a hover-pedi. He ran to the door. Something was flying away from a high floor, very fast. Jordan hacked into its directional coordinates. It was headed toward the old party district.

One of the cannons whirred in its direction.

"Don't fire!" Jordan cried.

He hopped on his pedi. It rose.

"I'll take this one myself."

And he sped away.

33

When Leonard saw the phalanx moving forward, he panicked. So he sniped, killing his first human. And the soldiers went predictably berserk. Most people on Earth had never known the terrors of war. But Leonard did now. He'd caused a massacre, but he had only one choice: escape.

Leonard called up his pedi and launched himself from a high window. By the time they noticed him, he was nearly over the horizon. He didn't know exactly where to go. Warning the people at the Blind Pig seemed like the right thing to do. But then again, he didn't want Captain Ted to escape or survive or do any more damage. On the other hand, he wasn't so into being ruled by the bloodless drones of the MDC, either.

Jordan's pedi went twice as fast as Leonard's, and he had about forty times the armor. Leonard swerved left, but he was driving a taxi, whereas the other guy had a seventy-million-credit intergalactic assault bike. Leonard swerved right. Jordan stayed with him. Leonard didn't want to dip down. He wasn't going to be able to control the pedi at this speed near the ground. Up wasn't much of an option, either. He'd stayed alive thus far because he could stay calm. That was his main strength as an action pilot, and as a person in general.

Jordan was stronger.

"STAND DOWN!" he shouted from his uniform's built-in broadcaster, "OR FACE THE WRATH OF THE MDC."

Leonard flipped him the finger. Jordan sped up alongside him, swerved left, and bashed the front of his bike into the passenger side of the pedi. The pedi made a whining noise, sparks flew, and it started to smoke. It hiccupped once in the air as it hovered, and then it began to drop toward the earth, nose first. Leonard snapped loose his buckle and pressed the button for his automatic door. But the pedi's systems had failed. Leonard swung around in the seat as the bike screamed toward the ground. He kicked both feet hard against the passenger side.

"Graaaaaaaaah!" he shouted as the door snapped off his hinges. Leonard launched himself from his seat. It was way down, but if he twisted his posture, maybe he could survive without permanent paralysis. He angled his body and closed his eyes.

His arm jerked upward. He felt something wrench in his socket, and he howled. The MDC pilot had grabbed his hand. Leonard looked down. He was flying maybe a hundred feet from surface level, hanging like a pendulum. It felt like something had torn permanently in his arm. The pain was so intense that—

♦ ♦ ♦

Some unknown time later, Leonard stirred. His mouth felt like it was full of dust. Everything on Mars did, all the time. His arm felt numb, but he could move it, surprisingly. A man hovered above him, holding a needle.

"Battlefield medicine," he said. "The best."

Leonard smacked his lips. "Thirsty," he said.

The man walked over to his hover-pedi and got a canteen. He bent down over Leonard and placed the canteen between his lips. Leonard gulped like he'd never had water before.

"Is that better?" the man said.

"Yeah," said Leonard. "My arm still hurts a little."

"Open up," the man said.

He slid a wafer into Leonard's mouth.

"This is a hundred thousand milligrams of indica extract. The strongest painkiller ever devised. It'll hold you for twenty-four hours until we can get you treated. You'll probably even be able to move that arm."

Leonard felt the wafer dissolve. The THC began to work within seconds. He sat up. He could even move his arm a bit. Marijuana made an excellent battlefield analgesic.

"Thanks, Jordan," he said, and then he realized what he'd said. "Jordan! Wow!"

"Nice to see you, too," Jordan said.

"What the fuck have you been doing?"

"Crystal pumped me full of drugs and brainwashed me through superintense paramilitary training."

"That sounds about right," Leonard said, never surprised by anything.

Jordan asked, "And why are you assassinating soldiers from the top floors of abandoned high-rises?"

"I got caught up in this revolution deal because it was cheap, but then I made a promise to someone as she died in my lap. So I kind of had to."

They looked at each other.

"Pretty fucking dramatic, huh?" Leonard said. "Total space adventure."

"Yeah, man," said Jordan.

But this wasn't something they were enjoying on their holo-watches. They were actually living it, however improbably. As a reminder, they saw a half dozen hover-pedis streaming across the horizon. Jordan's troopers had been released from their moorings. Jordan checked his coordinates.

"They're headed for a place called the Black Pig," Jordan said.

"That's a dive bar where the rebels are headquartered," Leonard said. "You've got at least forty-five heavily armed insurgents in that place."

"My men will blow the shit out of them," Jordan said.

"Maybe or maybe not."

"It's in the middle of a residential neighborhood," Jordan said.

"Yeah, one for *rich* people," Leonard said.

"They're still *people*, for Gaia's sake," said Jordan. "They don't deserve to die in a bloody turf battle just because they live in mixed-use condo developments. These men have been watching their friends get slaughtered for weeks. They are thirsty for blood and they don't care."

His eyes filling with the sincerity and righteousness that had been missing ever since he'd gotten to Mars, Jordan looked at Leonard.

Leonard knew that look. "Oh no," he said.

"Leonard!" Jordan said. "We have to stop this war!"

"I'm done with it already. Let them kill one another."

"No, we have to. It's up to us. We have the skills . . ." He fired his wrist cannon across a vacant lot, sending up a big puff of shrapnel smoke. "We have the technology. Most of all, we have the knowledge of a better way. Of the Earth way. Of a way where people can live together in harmony and be happy with Enough."

Leonard sighed. "Fuck Gaia in both holes," he said. "Fine."

Jordan shouted into his Device. "Platoon stand down! I have captured the assassin. That is an order!"

"What?" Leonard said. "Don't rat me out, dude!"

"Just wait," Jordan said.

Off in the distance, the platoon halted.

"Sir," said one of them. "We received a tip on rebel headquarters, and we are headed to engage."

"Not until I order," Jordan said. "Stand down."

"With all due respect, sir, we're going to move ahead."

And they flew on.

"That is insubordinate!" Jordan said. "Halt!" To Leonard, he said, "I knew they were going to do that. They are morons. I'm going to need you to fly this thing. Can you?"

"Dude, I'm a professional hover-pedi pilot."

"This is pretty high-tech."

"I can fly anything," Leonard said.

"Get on, then."

Leonard got into the pilot's seat, feeling woozy. He had maybe 50 percent mobility in his damaged arm. Jordan climbed on behind him.

"Shit," Leonard said. "How do you fly this thing?"

Jordan reached around and pushed a red button.

"Start with start," he said.

"Right," Leonard said.

The pedi lurched forward.

"It's impulse controlled," Jordan said. "Almost like thoughts, but through your Devices."

"So I fly this by . . . using the Force?" Leonard said, referring to ancient entertainment texts.

"Not exactly," said Jordan. "It doesn't work without wearable tech. But it has been developed to fly according to brainwaves."

"I know hundreds of people who eat garbage every day, and you get to fly this."

"That's why we fight, my friend," said Jordan. "So everyone can have Enough."

Leonard thought hard. The pedi ripped forward. Jordan almost flung off the back.

"Woot!" Leonard exclaimed.

"Just focus on moving toward those six bikes. Don't worry, this one is faster."

"Um, OK, Commander," said Leonard.

"Don't call me that."

"It's just funny because on Earth you used to dither around for hours deciding whether or not to 3-D print pizza or ramen. You'd be whining, like, 'Ewww, do they have too many carbs?' "

"Carbs are bad for you," Jordan said. "Just fly, Leonard."

"Roger that."

The bike tore away. Leonard steadied it. Behind him, Jordan mounted a portable stun cannon on his shoulder.

"Holy shit," Leonard said. "That's some real weaponry."

"The best the slave mines of Luna can buy."

He took aim with his helmet visor and squeezed off six shots. Four of them found their marks. The soldiers fell off their pedis. They dropped like branches blown off a tree. They weren't necessarily dead. The MDC had developed its armor to be immune from a single shot. But a fall at high speeds could have killed them. Maybe they could have activated the crash functions in their armor, which would provide extra padding. Jordan glanced behind him and saw at least a couple of them squirming around the ground. He wasn't sure about the others and probably never would be.

The remaining two pilots realized what was going on and started to maneuver, buzzing toward the city like bees. They had arrived in the pig-shit districts, where the lower-middle class could still afford houses. Within three minutes, they would be in mixed-use condo town, more densely populated and made from cheaper materials.

Jordan needed to connect now, to reduce collateral damage.

He fired twice. One hit, stopping the biker, while another sailed into the distance. Leonard sped up until Jordan and the last bike were parallel.

"Stand down!" Jordan shouted.

The biker accelerated. Leonard drew back alongside him and maintained speed. The biker pulled out a stun pistol. A shield flashed out of Jordan's wrist. The bullet twanged away. Jordan pressed down on Leonard's shoulders, stood up, and leapt onto the other bike, behind the pilot, who tried to swat him away. The bike veered. Jordan threw the pilot off, grabbing the handlebars. And he brought the bike to heel.

Leonard stopped. "Look at you," he said. "All grown up."

"Not by choice, believe me," Jordan said.

They flew on, side-by-side, for another three minutes, to the front door of the Black Pig. A dozen sadistic-looking clowns were standing out front, chugging from bottles and brandishing weapons.

"Oh, for Gaia's sake," said Jordan.

"Welcome to my world," Leonard said.

34

Jordan and Leonard looked at each other.

"We can do this," Leonard said.

"OK," Jordan said. "But no more killing. We are not killers."

"Follow my lead," Leonard said. He grabbed Jordan around the neck and began dragging him toward the door of the MDC. "Get out of my way! I have captured a prisoner!"

The punk clowns blocked the door. Nickel came out of the pack, hungry for more.

"I want to see Captain Ted."

"Captain Ted is busy right now, oy!" he said. "He's got appointments."

"This is a commander of the MDC!" said Leonard. "A valuable hostage."

"I'll never bow down to your kind!" Jordan said melodramatically.

"Let me see Ted now," Leonard said.

"Oi said he's busy!"

The clowns rattled their chains.

Jordan whispered in Leonard's ear, "Get ready."

Jordan spun out of Leonard's grasp, crouched low, and dropped two of the clowns with a low, sweeping kick. He pulled a stun pistol out of his boot and smacked darts into both their foreheads, which would find them waking up in an MDC dungeon while awaiting trial. When he said "no more killing," he meant it.

Leonard, meanwhile, less skilled in hand-to-hand combat, had flung himself against Nickel's chest. The clown clamped him there with one arm and pulled a knife from his belt with the other. Leonard stopped his hand before Nickel connected. But Nickel was stronger.

Jordan stunned Nickel with a blow to the neck, then flattened him with a sharp elbow to the face. The other ten or so clowns looked a little confused about what to do next.

"Does anyone else want to wake up in a cell?" Jordan said.

"Um, no?"

"Too bad," he said, and fired off a rapid volley of shots, dropping them each in turn.

On the third floor, Leonard spotted the glint of a sniper's rifle, turned, and fired. A clown teetered, twisted, and then fell out of the window.

"You're good at distance," Jordan said.

"I guess so," Leonard said.

Jordan talked into his wrist. "I've got thirteen enemy combatants down at the Black Pig," he said. "Request backup. Stun only."

"The last thing we need is more troops," Leonard said.

"That was a municipal wavelength," said Jordan. "Just a haul job, no SWAT."

"Look at us, the enforcers," said Leonard.

Fifteen minutes later, a sonic cannon blew open a twenty-foot hole in the front of The Black Pig. Fifty New Austin municipal officers walked through, along with Jordan and Leonard.

There were at least two dozen clowns in there, partying hard, rocking their heads off. Jordan raised a stun machine to the sky and rattled off a couple of rounds.

"Listen up!" he said. "This war is officially over! Give up your arms now, and you will not be directly prosecuted."

There was a pause. The bartender reached below the bar. Jordan sprayed him. The other clowns stood and started firing wildly. Two officers were hit, and dropped. The rest sprayed the bar with thousands of stun bullets. Many of them found a mark. Within seconds, everyone was dropped and snoozing on the floor of the bar.

Someone threw a sonic knife from behind the bar. It burrowed itself in the armor plate of Jordan's right shoulder.

"Ach," Jordan cried. That stung.

Leonard vaulted over the bar. The clown cringed, the last of the Mohawkans. Leonard blew a dart. The clown collapsed. The revolution had been defeated.

"I'm not bad up close, either," he said.

Jordan had removed his shoulder plate. There was a huge red welt, but his skin had held.

There was a buzzing sound over the bar. Everyone looked at the buzzer. It buzzed again. Then more loudly and more insistently, over and over again, like a nagging fly.

"That's coming from upstairs," Leonard said. "Captain Ted must be out of THC chips."

The buzzer buzzed.

"Someone has to bring them to him," Leonard said, "or he will never stop nagging."

Jordan turned to the cops. "Clean this place up," he said. "Check around the neighborhood and make sure there wasn't any collateral damage to person or property. Leonard, come up the stairs with me. What can we expect up there?"

"Last time I saw, it was an old man getting blown by three drugged-out sycophants."

"Ew."

"Windowless room, apparently unvented."

"Oh, man."

They went up the stairs. When Jordan kicked in the door, they found Captain Ted alone in bed, sitting upright, wearing a robe, reading a hardback book. There was a bottle of bourbon on the nightstand, but it was mostly full. The room did smell like weed and farts, though.

He looked at them over the top of his readers. "What the fuck is going on, Tolliver?" he said.

"Didn't you hear what was going on downstairs?" Leonard said.

"Nah, my hearing's shot."

"They blew out the front wall of the bar!"

"What?"

"Didn't you feel the vibrations?"

"This place is always vibrating; that's why it's the best! That's why it's going to be the city hall of the New New Austin!"

"It's over, Captain," Leonard said. "Your troops are routed. The MDC has laid them out."

"Fucking fascists!" Captain Ted said. He tried to struggle to his feet, but that seemed like a lot of work. He slumped back on the bed. "We will finish them all!" he said when he was done.

"No," said a voice behind Jordan. "The fascists win again."

Jordan looked around.

There stood Dick Waters and Crystal.

"I can't let you in, sir," Jordan said. "It's a security breach."

"Let them pass!" said Captain Ted. "I know that voice. Come in here, Waters. I want to spit in your fucking face."

"Do what your father says, Jordan," Waters said.

Jordan cocked his head but let them through. "Father?" he said to Waters, and then to the Captain, "Who are you?"

"I'm Captain Ted," he said. "Always have been in my heart. But they used to call me Ruben Kincaid."

Dick Waters lunged for Captain Ted's bed, his hands extended, eyes wild and puffy. Leonard and Jordan restrained him.

"You sonofabitch!" he shouted. "You murdered everybody! You ruined everything! You destroyed the whole goddamn city."

"Don't be so touchy, Dick," said the captain.

"I will kill you!"

"*Dad?*" Jordan said.

Captain Ted sighed. "What?" he said.

"You left!" Jordan said. "You left . . ."

"A long time ago," said Captain Ted.

"You told Mom you were going to come back."

"I was."

"She thinks you're dead."

"I am. Or at least the person she knew. I was reborn as"—he held his saggy arms wide—"this."

"You left me!" Jordan said. "Didn't you care about me at all?"

"He's not going to care about anything!" said Dick Waters, still thrashing in Jordan and Leonard's grasp. "He is going to be dead. Right now."

"Just try it, old man," said Captain Ted, trying once again to stand up, and this time standing tall.

"I'm not going to do it," said Waters. He looked at Jordan. "*He* is."

35

"I can't kill him," Jordan said. "He's my *father*. Apparently."

"You will do what I pay you to do," said Waters.

"For the last time," Jordan said. "*You don't pay me!*"

"We don't?" He turned to Crystal. "We're supposed to pay our employees, right?"

"Jordan is remunerated in other ways, Daddy," she said. "I'm holding his money in a trust."

"Typical Jordan," said Captain Ted.

"What?" Jordan said.

"Always overeager. Always someone's patsy. Never his own person. I remember as a kid how eager you were to please, what a sucker you were. I could tell you to do anything, and you would have done it. You always followed, never led."

Jordan's eyes were getting teary. "But . . ."

"Very typical of the son of a great man. Very hard for you, I know. I remember one time I took you to the holo-mall, you were probably about five, and you were clinging to me and smiling and laughing, and I thought, 'What a disgusting little sycophant.'"

"You left me!"

"That's right," Captain Ted said. "I left you in the holo-mall. I left you for hours. And did you cry for me? No. Did you look for me? No. There you were in the food-generation area, happily playing with other kids, not worrying about anything, just following the herd, never standing up for what is yours. You were a great disappointment to me, Jordan. In every way. It made it easy to leave and never come back."

"Kill him!" said Dick Waters. "You can't let him talk to you that way."

"I won't do it," Jordan said, though his hand found his stun pistol.

"Why not, Jordan?" said Captain Ted. "Why stop taking orders now? You've always been so compliant, so eager to buttress the established order. There's not a rebellious tendon in your body, you weak, second-rate tool of the state! So do it, kill me. Kill me!"

"No!"

"Blow my fucking brains out, you third-rate Earth scum! Do it!"

A shot rang out. Captain Ted stared ahead blankly, a bullet lodged in his brain. He collapsed to the floor.

Jordan looked over to Leonard, who was holding his pistol up. It smoked.

"Your dad was a jerk," he said.

Jordan didn't feel sad, or happy, particularly. He hadn't traveled millions of miles so he could journey back to a past where Daddy didn't love him. Mostly, he felt gratitude toward his friend.

"Is he dead?" said Dick Waters.

"It appears so," said Crystal.

"So it's over?"

"Yes."

"Hah!" Waters said. "Then I win! I win! I win everything! I win all of Mars!"

He started to dance.

"I am the king of Mars!" he said. "Undisputed and forever. Ha ha ho hee hee!"

Waters's daughter and Jordan and Leonard looked at him incredulously.

"Forever and ever!" Waters said. "I was right, Ted was wrong, capitalism does work, it will triumph. The land is ours to take!"

"I don't know if this is the time, Daddy," Crystal said.

"No! It is the time! Now we're going to build. *Really* build. Higher and higher, more and more expensive, and nothing is going to stop us! The revolution is dead and the people, whoever they are, lose. I was right, I was always right, so now let's—"

Another shot rang out. Another bullet buried itself in another forehead. Jordan's gun was smoking.

"Your dad was a jerk," he said to Crystal.

She studied him coolly. "He was," she said. "And he had to be stopped at some point. But still, you murdered him."

"Technically," said Jordan, "it was in the heat of battle."

"That's not going to fly," Crystal said.

Jordan wondered if he was going to have to shoot her, too.

She sighed. "Look, I'm not happy he's dead," she said. "I'm very upset, can't you see?"

She didn't look particularly upset.

"But I also recognize that this is politically convenient for me. Let's just say they shot each other," she said. "No one's going to dispute that. No matter how weird the ballistics look. And I control the media, so there won't be any questions of me while I'm in deep mourning for my dear dead daddy."

Crystal planted pistols in Captain Ted's and Dick Waters's hands. The scandalous story of their horrifying death duel would come out soon enough. For now, the three of them left them there and went downstairs, where police crews were busy cleaning up the mess, dragging out the bodies of drugged clown rebels, and sweeping up shattered whiskey bottles.

Crystal sat on a bar stool, between Jordan and Leonard. She pulled a joint out of her pocket, lit it, puffed, and passed it left. Jordan and Leonard took equally eager tokes.

"Dude," she said.

"Man," said Leonard. "What a ride."

"I'm still very conflicted," said Jordan.

Crystal said, "Don't you ever relax?"

"This is what he's like," said Leonard.

"Great," Jordan said. "Now they're dead. Now what? This city is a total mess."

"Any suggestions?" said Crystal.

"Well," said Leonard, "people definitely shouldn't eat garbage."

"Agreed."

"And they shouldn't drink their own pee."

"We get it, Leonard," Jordan said. "It comes down to this: The revolution got out of control. Violence isn't the answer. But at the core, they are right. This city has gotten too expensive. No one is saying you should close down all the clubs and restaurants. They're fun. You need music and art and all the rest.

"And there's no reason to shut down business and development entirely, either. But you also need to make sure that everyone has an affordable place to live, and safe, decent schools to send their kids to that don't just teach MDC propaganda, and good access to transportation, and healthy food to eat. You might not want to hear it, but people really do need to have Enough. If they have Enough, then most of them will be happy most of the time."

Crystal was quiet a moment, as though this had never occurred to her before. Then she gave a shrug of her own.

"I can make that happen," she said.

"There you go."

"Daddy never would have done it. Which is why his death is so convenient. I look forward to working with you to make it happen."

"Oh, I don't want to stay," Jordan said.

"What?"

"I didn't want to come to Mars in the first place, and it's been nothing but a messed-up nightmare for me. I want my freedom."

"Jordan, I don't think—"

"I want two billion credits, tax free, and I want my criminal record on Earth expunged so I can move freely among the continents and planets as I see fit. I also want a Highest Honor commendation on my digital résumé. Make me look good in case I ever decide I want to work again. I have served you well and loyally in every possible way. And I deserve this."

Crystal took a toke. "OK," she said.

"Seriously?"

"I would have done it months ago," she said, "but you didn't ask."

"So that's it?"

"I'm gonna need a couple of hours to move around some encrypted files," she said. "But yeah, not a problem. What about your friend?"

"What do you want to do, Leonard?" Jordan asked.

"Huh?" Leonard said. "Sorry. I was spacing out."

"Are you coming with me?"

"Where are you going?"

"Somewhere I can be free."

"Sure. I've got nothing here. Literally nothing. These clothes I'm wearing are the only thing I have, and they are all burnt."

"Two billion credits for my friend, too," Jordan said.

"He can have five hundred million," said Crystal. "Considering he was a high-ranking deputy in a terrorist organization."

"Not on purpose."

"Regardless. I don't think he's earned the same salary as you."

"Five hundred million credits?" Leonard said. "I can support myself for five years on that."

"OK, then." Crystal stood up and took Jordan's hand. "Thank you for your service, Commander Kincaid."

"Thank you for *your* service," said Jordan, then pulled her close to him and gave her a long, deep kiss.

"I wish I had someone to kiss," Leonard said.

But he didn't.

♦ ♦ ♦

Crystal Waters stood in her penthouse, looking out over the city, which was still smoking in places but was otherwise calm. The lights had begun to turn on again. She had reopened the flight paths. Restaurants had begun to put out their specials. Slowly, the noise was beginning to rise.

She'd been waiting for her father to die. It had merely happened a little ahead of schedule. It would take her a few months, maybe a year, to rebuild the area around the ruined towers. That had been her plan all along. There was plenty of space out there, and also out by the soybean fields, to build villages of decent, affordable housing, and neighborhood schools that weren't run by morons. Daddy had only been able to see temporary profit in a small-scale landgrab. His vision stopped at the borders of the dome. Hers didn't.

When she was a girl, Crystal would gaze at the stars and think, *I'm going to make so much money off real estate when I grow up*. Beyond the dome, beyond the red dust and blue sunset, lay a vast planet that held infinite riches. Crystal Waters wanted to take them. The MDC had barely begun to develop that land.

Crystal had big plans for Mars.

Meanwhile, Jordan and Leonard, their records clean and their bank accounts and bellies full, were cruising in the elite lane on their hovercycles, toward the spaceport. They both had the cycles on autopilot and were kicking back in celebration.

"Mars wasn't so bad," Leonard said.

"Are you kidding?" said Jordan. "It was hell."

"What are you talking about? We picked up some serious skills here. On Earth we couldn't do anything. Now you're a bad-ass space ninja and I am a sniper."

"That is true," Jordan said.

"We did it! We came to Mars looking for some action."

"I wasn't looking for any action."

"Yeah, but you found it anyway. And you got laid, too."

"All right, fine. But I'm going to lay off the drugs for a while," Jordan said. "I don't mind having fighting and weapons and piloting skills and some excellent sexual experience. But I would like to be able to experience normal human emotions again."

"Fair enough. I'll give up drugs, too. Drugs suck."

"Yeah."

"Except for weed."

"That goes without saying. It's from the Earth."

Leonard sparked a joint. He took a puff and passed it to Jordan, who took his own long, smooth drag.

"So what do you want to do now?" Leonard asked.

Jordan wasn't sure. He just wanted affordable housing in a fun place to live. That had to exist somewhere. He said, "I hear Venus is pretty cool."

ABOUT THE AUTHOR

Photo © 2013 John Keatley

Neal Pollack is an American satirist, novelist, short-story writer, and journalist. Pollack has written nine previous books: *The Neal Pollack Anthology of American Literature*, *Never Mind the Pollacks*, *Beneath the Axis of Evil*, *Alternadad*, *Stretch*, *Jewball*, *Downward-Facing Death*, *Open Your Heart*, and *Repeat*. He's also a three-time *Jeopardy!* champion, Pollack lives in Austin, Texas, with his wife and son.